DEATH HOUSE

I could piece together no clear picture of what was going on in this mansion. It looked like an elegant hotel, not a well-known sanitarium. There were few people here other than the man who invited me, who claimed to know me, yet I had no memory of him. He was a physician. His clinic should have been a refuge for the sick, but a woman called it a death house.

I was weary, tense, overreacting, I told myself. I should return to my room and rest . . .

I moved toward the door to find my way back; my footsteps filled the small room with sound. Like the house, it was a strange room. It had no furniture, no windows, only big heavy draperies.

And, yes, a coffin.

WALTZ IN THE SHADOWS

A spellbinding gothic novel by the author of
The Shadow of the Raven

† † †

By Catherine Rieger from The Berkley Publishing Group

THE SHADOW OF THE RAVEN

WALTZ IN THE SHADOWS

CATHERINE RIEGER

JOVE BOOKS, NEW YORK

WALTZ IN THE SHADOWS

A Jove Book / published by arrangement with
the author

PRINTING HISTORY
Jove edition / December 1993

ISBN: 0-515-11254-2

A JOVE BOOK®
Jove Books are published by The Berkley Publishing Group,
200 Madison Avenue, New York, New York 10016.
JOVE and the "J" design
are trademarks belonging to Jove Publications, Inc.

PRINTED IN THE UNITED STATES OF AMERICA

10 9 8 7 6 5 4 3 2 1

For Wolfram,
husband, healer, hero at both.

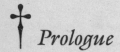# *Prologue*

Philadelphia
Summer, 1888

Again I was plunged into that deep, dark void, black and formless, without window or door. Space had no meaning, and time did not exist in this wasteland. I heard only fevered whispers.

Tortures of the dark they were, these demons of my sleep.

Voices . . . treacherous voices.

"He stole. He's a cheat."

"No," I cried. "My father is an honest man. A good physician."

"People won't forget. You'll be disgraced."

"Shame!"

Again I shouted, "No!"

Loathsome faces bore down on me. "Then save yourself. Tell him you're against him."

"Never."

"We will tell him."

"Don't," I begged. "It's a lie.

"Papa, they lied.

"Papa," I called. I called him again. "Papa? Answer me."

I raised his head, his lifeless limbs. Saw the small brown vial, uncapped and empty, upon his nightstand.

"No!" I screamed, my face brushing back and forth across the pillow. "No!"

1

Bolting upright in my bed, I was stiff with fear, sweaty, cold, and trembling. I reached to my night table with a shaking hand and quickly closed it around the little velvet box that held a medal.

Keep it as a souvenir, sweet Emily.

Father's voice! Clear as the summer day we dug up the war memento near the battlefield at Gettysburg. A lifetime ago, it seemed.

I raised the lid, removed the medallion, and traced its circular shape with a loving finger as tears burned my cheeks. "I wish I could have helped you, Papa," I whispered despairingly, for the need to right the past wrongs would never leave me.

Again my hand searched the nightstand.

Was the letter that came from Europe today real? Or was that, too, a dream, a new twist in this fiendish nightmare? Fumbling for matches, my fingers nearly knocked over the glass chimney of the lamp. I struck a light and immediately looked for the envelope with foreign postage. I unfolded the paper, my eyes moving quickly across the lettering, once, twice.

Yes, it was true! Dr. Franz Joseph Demel, a colleague of my father, wanted me to come to Vienna to help write Papa's biography. I had been there once with him. Strange, I could not remember this Dr. Demel, but I would go again. I would honor my father and expose his jealous enemies who killed him and manipulated me. With anger, hot and raw, I thought of how they harassed me, pushed me out of the medical world.

And I wondered again if they would have done this if I had been willing to lie or if I had been born a man.

I would tell all in this biography, and in the telling seek my peace.

He that deceives, himself deceived shall be.

CHAUCER

✝ Chapter One

Vienna,
Late summer, 1888

The fog crept silently upward from the Danube to wrap the city in pale, thin shrouds. No lamplighter appeared to brighten the way, and not a window welcomed the traveler.

There were only shadows. And mist!

Its restless tendrils stretched along the darkening length of backways and alleys, catching on the bricks of the tenements and factories like threads of gauze upon open sores.

The coachman glanced back, unsettling me further with his shrewd smile. "Almost there," he shouted.

He had to be wrong. Or mad. Nothing about the city seemed familiar—not the stench, the squalor, or the soot. Where was the fabled Ringstrasse, the grand circular boulevard where one went to promenade, watch the fashionable people, see the magnificent palace and all the splendid buildings? What lay left and right in this dreary evening in September was a city, or part of one, gripped miserably by decay and gloom.

The carriage rattled over the ruts in the narrow road, and, as we came toward an intersection, I saw a pinpoint of light. It grew larger as we approached, revealing a man pulling a cart piled high with what appeared to be beds, chairs, chests, huge bundles tied with ropes, and buckets or pots—all manner of possessions. His wife and children walked on either side of the wagon. As my carriage passed, they raised their arms and shouted. My coachman yelled back, and then something hard hit my window, cracking it. I turned abruptly away, fearful of this sharp and untoward threat.

Once more my driver looked back and down. He held a lantern, and by its light I again saw his saturnine grin. A ripple of fear washed through me, causing the dark sights and sounds to echo and grow in my mind. Hellish whispers of the night they were, and I gripped the armrest so hard, my fingers turned numb.

I shuddered, wondering anew at his questionable choice of routes. Not having been in Vienna since I was twelve, some ten years before, I was appalled at the living conditions of its poor. If I had had any exposure to such in my youth, I must have repressed it, for, on my life, I could not remember anything of it.

Another dark street. A second laden cart, a horse-drawn one. Then a third crossed our path and rattled away, leaving a plume of dust to mix with the fog.

The relentless gray haze coiled about our conveyance as it clacked and jolted along. Then the ride grew smoother and more tolerable. We were free of the rutted track, the shameful misery, and, to some extent, the fog. We were climbing steadily now, and I held aside the leather curtain to venture another look at my surroundings. These were more in keeping with my memories. Modest houses and a church nestled into a softly rolling Alpine foothill. I dared to open my window. To my surprise I heard whistling from the coachman's seat, a tune not unpleasant with the rhythm of the prancing hooves. Passersby stopped, promenaders smiled. The carriage slowed and drifted toward a wine garden by the roadside where I would like to have stopped, for in such a garden I used to sit with my father.

Strawberry phosphate.

That is what he had always ordered for me. On sabbatical from his medical practice in Philadelphia, he had studied in Vienna ten years ago. And now, just a year after his death, I was returning to the city on a compelling mission. So close was I to my father, so much did I revere him, that I jumped at the opportunity to immortalize him.

The Demel house was outside the city, tucked into the Viennese woods. According to its owner, it was a private clinic similar to the one my father planned to have, had he lived. That was another inducement. I would feel comfortable in such surroundings, quite in my element. I had helped my father with his patients in recent summers and had studied at medical school. Forced to leave that, I had worked in an asylum in Philadelphia.

There were no café gardens now. No strollers. Only steep meadows, vague tree lines in ever-upward ascent, and a cool breeze. And the whistling. But that ceased, too, when the carriage slowed and made a wide circling turn at a pair of majestic iron gates. Passing through them, I saw an oversized gilded *D* on the ornate grillwork. The coachman turned to me and pointed at the letter. *Did he say Devil?*

I must have misunderstood, I thought, with a choked laugh. Most surely it was Demel. On the coachman drove, along a winding pebbled drive, and then quite suddenly he drew the carriage to a stop.

The light was rapidly waning, but it was not too dark to gain an impression of grandeur. The expansive grounds appeared intricately designed, the imposing mansion was ornate . . . and something else I could only sense at this hour. For that dusky rose that softens the end of the day was fading strangely here, giving way to a soulless twilight. This was journey's end.

Dressed stunningly in black and gold, a footman greeted me with a nod and escorted me to a massive door which swung open silently at my approach. A butler appeared and bowed. None of this came back to me. Hard as I searched the dimmest recess of my mind, I could not remember being here. Ever. Yet, in his letter Professor Doctor Demel implied that he knew me, that I had visited him with my father. Not here, though. Not even once.

"Miss Hopkins, Miss Emily Hopkins," said a well-modulated voice, not the butler's.

I turned and faced a man who was tall, slim, and gray-haired. A man of impeccable bearing. Dismissing the servant with a barely perceptible shift of his eyes, he moved toward me in smooth, fluid strides. His dark eyes were quickly assessive, approving, I thought. Each gesture and expression was touched with grace. Releasing a clutched breath, I said, "Yes, are you Dr. Demel?"

"Indeed," he said with a laugh. "And I am delighted to see you again."

Shaking his hand, I allowed myself to be brought farther into the foyer. "Come in, come in, my dear. You must be weary."

I heard a faint note of concern in his voice which prompted me to study my host more carefully; the full head of hair waved silkily back, the long, thin face and hawkish nose, lips tightly curved in a measured smile. Finally I looked into his eyes to gauge his sincerity. Black and flashing, they were unusual eyes. Piercing, yet kindly, they were full of contrast. Surely I would have remembered this man. "Yes," I replied, deciding to agree with what I could. "It was a long journey." And worth it, I silently added, for a favorable biography would honor my father.

I glanced about, trying to spring the lock on my memory, but to no avail. Neither the rich Persian carpets, the grand sweep of marble staircase, nor the elegantly appointed reception rooms, left and right, triggered a remembrance.

"Something wrong, Miss Hopkins?"

"No . . . I . . . I'm fatigued. That's all."

"Of course." He took my hand and pressed it between his thin fingers. "You are so kind to come. We will make every attempt to make your stay—" He paused and looked at me with a wide, penetrating gaze that drew me into those dark pools. "Memorable. Most memorable, Miss Hopkins. Now, Hans," he said, turning to the butler, "let's see to our guest's comfort."

A girl several years my younger appeared momentarily. She wore a dark gray dress and a dust cap and apron trimmed with lace. Sophie was her name, and I followed her up the stairs and down a long corridor with numbered rooms. Convinced now that I had never been here, I thought that I must not have met the doctor at his villa, but somewhere in the city, perhaps while I was out walking with my father or having cake with him in a café. Dr. Demel obviously kept in touch with my father over the years because the man knew of my interest in my father's work.

Papa had specialized in problems of the nerves. He worked with a number of patients who suffered from neurasthenia, weak nerves. Like many American physicians, he had studied in Europe. Vienna, especially, was a seedbed for theories that recognized the value of psychological factors in illness. But European doctors learned much from their American colleagues about the treatment of such afflictions in hospitals. My father had had significant experience training personnel in larger settings. In fact, Dr. Demel's letter of invitation referred to my father's expertise and requested that I bring Papa's journals because they describe plans for his own clinic.

We went up another flight of steps, then down an interminable passageway. I had to walk quickly to keep up with the efficient Sophie. Along she glided, pointing to paintings on the wall, explaining some things about the family. The pace was rapid, the faces a blur of features and personalities. On she went until she reached a large door.

"They live in this wing," she said with puzzling terseness.

We passed a drawing room that was well lit and obviously occupied. Angry voices from inside it poured through the partially opened door, following us to my suite across the hall. My room was most appealing, but when Sophie left, my curiosity was engaged more by the heated discussion, which I could not help but overhear, than by my lovely new quarters.

"I must be among the first to have them, Max," the woman said with aggressive petulance. "My house will glow like the Ringstrasse itself."

"A few lights, perhaps. You don't need electricity in every single room. Besides, you'll delay your move if you continue to make new demands on the workmen." The man had a remarkable speaking voice. Its depth and clarity gave it a pleasingly rich and balanced quality. "God knows," he continued, "you can't wait to get away from me fast enough."

"Surely you can do something to prevent the builders' foot-dragging," she snapped. "I want to have a housewarming the week the new Burgtheater opens." Her voice grew shrill. "In my apartment. Mine. Where I can do what I want, when I please."

There was a long, strained silence. "Don't neglect 'with whom you please,' Iris. It's unlike you to spare me a single infidelity."

"Don't be tiresome, Maximillian. For years I've dreamed of living on the Ringstrasse. And with the gala opening not far off, the timing's perfect."

"And Peter?"

"What about him?"

"Have you given any thought to how another separation will affect him? The child is pale and thin. While you live the high life in Paris and London, he barely eats. He misses you."

"Nonsense. His eating problems have nothing to do with me. I had breakfast with him this morning, and he barely touched his food."

"He's afraid his mother will leave again."

"Well, if he misses me so, all the more reason he should move to the Ringstrasse with me and not stay here in this . . . this godforsaken house with you."

I heard a chair scrape angrily against the floor. Even when he sounded frustrated, there was obvious dignity in this man's tone. "Go with your friends, Iris. Prattle on about your ball gowns. Compare the latest perversions in dog breeding, for all I care." His tone was laced with sarcasm. "A useless life is only an early death."

"Is that your beloved Goethe?" the woman asked. "That's your problem, Max. You're living in the wrong half of the century. You're out of step with the times. All Vienna is waltzing, and you've stuck your feet in a grave. That's what it's like here. A death house. It's depressing."

"Life is not a gay waltz for everyone, dear wife. Ask the tenement dwellers in the Ottakring, or one of the patients here who's trapped by his own fears. Ask one of them if he feels like dancing. Tell me what he says."

"You too serious, Max. After you go to the theater, you have to discuss the play with your cronies until you've taken all the pleasure out of it."

"Why do you go to the theater?"

"To see and be seen. Why else?"

The man's sarcasm now was almost palpable. "Why else, indeed, Iris?"

I could not bear to hear any more. I reached for my shawl and ran down the hallway, a different way than I had come, I soon discovered. At a sharp turn I descended a narrow, dimly lit staircase with steep wooden steps. They creaked menacingly at the touch of my feet, and the noise was unsettling. It made me feel that I should not be here, that I was sneaking around, intruding in some private place. I had already overheard a nasty argument.

Where was everybody? I was bound to come upon someone, perhaps be discovered where I had no reason to be. So far I did not feel comfortable in this house. There was little to make me feel welcome. I quickened my footsteps and looked around. I saw nothing. No one. But I heard something. Hushed voices. Muffled sounds from heavy shoes. They were steadily approaching.

At the bottom of the stairs I turned right, away from the footsteps, and found myself in a high-walled vestibule of some sort. It was an odd room, small like a closet, with just one door. And it was empty except for voluminous draperies that covered one wall. Why those drapes attracted me, I cannot say, but I walked over and parted them with a quick hand.

No window!

The voices grew louder. So did the heavy shuffle.

I dashed behind the folds of fabric and held their ends so I could see out, yet still be concealed. A small procession approached. The men appeared to be carrying something cumbersome. They stopped at the door and turned slowly in the hallway, careful not to bump the walls. One was short. He shifted his burden with difficulty, then they entered. I bit my lips to stifle a cry.

The burly coachman led the trio. For a moment even he struggled with the long box that looked like a coffin. "Weighs more'n the last one," he said. "Let's get 'er down."

I let the draperies come together and pressed myself against the wall. From a room beyond the door I thought I heard another voice, but it was lost in the sudden thud before me.

" 'ave some respect for the dead, will ya?"

There was a coarse drunken laugh. A belch.

"Amen," said another irreverently.

I heard shuffling sounds again, receding into the hallway.

I remained perfectly still, not daring to move for several long minutes. Then I finally did look. The room was bare except for the coffin. Whose?

Leaving my hiding place, I walked around the box, fingering its rough wood. Death was a fact of life in a hospital, but the focus of the Demel establishment was not medical. It was a retreat for people with exhausted nerves. It promised a rest cure.

Of course someone could suddenly die. Yes, that's what must have happened. Yet the coachman had mentioned another death, referring to it almost jokingly. I began to wonder when that death had occurred.

I could piece together no clear picture of what was going on in this mansion. It looked like an empty elegant hotel, not a well-known sanitarium. There were few people here other than the man who invited me, who claimed to know me, yet, I had no memory of him. He was a physician. His clinic should have been a refuge for the sick, but a woman had called it a death house.

I was weary, tense, overreacting, I told myself. I should return to my room and rest. Perhaps everything would appear different in the morning. Then I would meet the family members, perhaps even the patients and staff. I would learn more about the villa and all its inhabitants. Someone would tell me about the death. Provide an explanation.

I moved toward the door to find my way back; my footsteps filled the small room with sound. Like the house, it was a strange room. It had no furniture, no windows, only big heavy draperies.

And, yes, a coffin.

✝ Chapter Two

I walked quickly down the hall, following the meager light, and went through another strange little room that led to a second dim corridor. It was long and arched, and at its end I came to a heavy door which opened to a courtyard. An old stable lantern swayed on a tree branch, and I wondered if I should take the lamp and make my way to the front entrance along the well-trodden track that appeared to parallel the configuration of the house, or if I should retrace my steps inside. As I stood debating, I became aware of the fragrance in the courtyard, the peace it seemed to offer, and, before I knew it, the door slipped quietly out of my fingers.

The scent of roses, the last of summer, filled the damp air. Drawn by this, I made my way along a shadowed path. I would enjoy what I could of the garden, for flowers were my weakness, then I would return to my room. But even as I thought this, I felt a niggling quiver of uncertainty. I had a strange feeling I was not alone. Something was close, too close. I paused to look, to listen. The night was still. On the edge of darkness.

Then I heard a stifled belch. I turned abruptly to go back, and as I did I thought I detected movement within the shadows. My heart gave a wild leap of fear, and I began to run. To my horror, the rough image began to take shape. With pounding heart, I saw a man lounging against a trellis. He was grinning.

"What's your name, miss?"

13

I tried to avoid him by stepping around the arch.

"What's your hurry?" said another, appearing suddenly from the side of the bushes.

In the restless swing of the lantern light I saw two of the trio carrying the coffin. I recognized their hats, smelled the whiskey on them, and saw their smiles, dark as the night itself. I glanced uneasily from one to the other, not knowing whether to go forward or retreat. The short one's bloated face came toward me slowly.

I felt my blood drain to my toes, and I started to run, but he grabbed my arm, twisting it behind my back. "We got somethin' real nice for ya, and you're rushin' off." He shook his head drunkenly. "Ain't very friendly."

"Let go of me," I shouted, struggling to get free.

"That's no way to handle a woman," the first crowed. He gave a short nasty laugh, bringing a bottle to his mouth. Then, as if he thought better of it, he set the liquor aside. "Hold her for me, Heinrich. I'm astride 'er first."

"No!" I screamed. "No!" I tried to tear myself loose from my captor, but my efforts caused my arm to be twisted harder. I kicked at him blindly, dropped the lantern, and heard the glass shatter. The vile man held both my wrists.

"Save your fight, missy, for somethin' better."

I could smell his foul breath, and I screamed in terror.

"Unhand that woman, or I'll beat you within an inch of your life," a commanding voice bellowed behind me.

I was instantly released.

"We were just havin' a little fun," the short man explained.

"Fun, you call it?" One savage fist sent the miscreant sprawling on the ground. "Pack your things, both of you, and don't let me see you near here again!"

There was no mistaking his voice. Despite its chilling tone, I recognized it as belonging to the man I had overheard fighting with his wife. He held up his lamp, and I watched my assailants study his large frame warily. Without another word they left, and the tall figure turned to me.

"Are you hurt?" he asked.

I shook my head, looking away.

"Are you sure?"

"Yes," I said, nodding, but now my eyes went to the face of my rescuer. Gone was the thundering anger, the raw disgust. Replacing them was worry tempered by compassion.

"Visiting hours are long since over," he said. "Would you like to come inside and wait for your carriage there?"

I must have looked confused. Then I realized he thought I was a family member visiting a patient.

"I'm Emily Hopkins," I said, hoping my name would identify me as an awaited guest at the villa, but I received, in turn, a bewildered look.

Several moments passed before I spoke. When I did, I felt myself trembling inside, for I wondered with growing apprehension why Dr. Demel had not told others of my arrival and purpose here. "I'm from America—Philadelphia, actually." I was about to tell him of my father's biography when I noticed his expression lighten with sudden recognition.

"Hopkins?" he repeated, enthused. "From Philadelphia?"

"Yes."

"I'm Dr. Schaller. Maximillian Schaller."

"Did you know my father, Dr. Samuel Hopkins?"

Maximillian did not answer. He chose, instead, to guide me toward the house. At the nearest entrance we went inside, and only there did he release his gentle hold on my arm.

"I knew only of your father." He paused, watching me keenly, deciding whether to go on. When he did, his voice was low, almost intimate. "Why did you come here, of all places?"

"To help with the biography," I replied, returning his scrutiny with a sense of alarm that made me feel weak.

"Whose?"

"My father's. Dr. Demel is writing a book about him. Didn't you know that?" It was only then I realized that perhaps Maximillian might not be aware of this fact. I knew nothing about him, nothing about his affiliation with the villa. I only knew he argued with his wife and came to my aid.

I liked his expressive face. It was virile, alert and knowing. But its contours, strong as they were, were not as compelling as his eyes; bold and blue, direct and intense, yet kind, they were alive with perception and rich with humor.

"The director of the clinic neglected to mention it to me," he said simply.

I began to wonder what he had meant when he'd said, "Here, of all places," but he spoke again so quickly and sympathetically that the thought vanished.

"What a terrible introduction you've had here," he said. Then rather nervously he took a few steps forward to adjust the wick in the lamp. He turned his attention to the clock and small bronze statue beside it, repositioning them twice. "Our apologies," he added, looking up. "Those men won't trouble you again."

"Thanks to you."

His eyes were on me fully now, studying my face quite openly. He smiled slowly, wonderfully, his blue eyes lighting with warmth. "Now, let me see to it that you are taken to the guest room," he said, reaching for the tassel on the bellpull.

"I've already been there."

He turned and looked surprised. "When?"

I flushed. Not wanting him to think I had overheard his argument with his wife, I answered, "A little while ago."

His wife. He was married. Dear God. I was blatantly admiring a man, a *married* man.

His expression turned quizzical. "I see."

But he did not see. Thank heavens he could not. I wondered fleetingly if I should have pretended I was a brief visitor, instead of a long-term guest. I wondered if I had made a mistake in coming here, if I should leave in the morning. My mind was reeling.

"Yes, Hannelore," I heard him say. "Please show Miss Hopkins to the guest suite."

I followed willingly, almost humbly, grateful it was Hannelore and not Sophie, the first maid I had met. How would I have explained my presence so far from my room?

A ridiculous thought. I'd never have to explain to a maid. She would not dare to ask. But by tomorrow she might learn of my assault and talk about it. I disliked gossip, hated it. I had been hurt by it once, so terribly pained I—

I had to calm down, get a good grip on myself, and I succeeded, to some extent, as I followed the quiet Hannelore through the empty corridors and up to the second landing. There I heard voices, cultured female voices.

"It is simply outrageous that a firm like Silber and Fleming can't get them. I'll not accept such incompetence."

Just then a plump woman stepped into the corridor. She looked ridiculous in a frilly pink confection and a wide-brimmed straw hat with floppy purple flowers. A fur piece, appearing very much like the dead animal it was, hung over one shoulder, adding to her comic entrance. She was working her fingers into long, kid gloves when she suddenly looked up and saw me. "Do you always stare?" she asked bluntly.

I blushed profusely, but recovered my grace by flattering her. "Only when admiring someone," I lied. The woman nodded and beamed, completely satisfied. I would have continued on my way if her companion had not detained me further.

"Who are you talking to, Tante Friedericke?"

"Oh, Iris," the grande dame trilled, "come meet our new guest."

Finally someone other than Dr. Demel did know of me.

"Guest?" came an imperial query. "Since when do we have guests without my knowledge?"

"Who are you?" Friedericke quietly whispered to me.

So Dr. Demel had not told her either. Another slight, but my surprise at this and the previous ones paled by comparison to the shock I felt when I saw Iris.

Out she came in a swirl of silk. I wondered why these two were dressed so formally, but the thought was instantly forgotten when I saw her face. The woman could have worn a penitent's sack and retained her appeal, for she was stunning.

"I'm Iris Schaller," she said, her bearing regal.

"And I'm Emily Hopkins. I have come from America to assist Professor Doctor Demel."

Both women looked puzzled. "Onkel Franz said nothing of this to me." The younger one shrugged. "No matter, I swear I'm the last to be told what goes on in my own home these days."

"You're never home, Iris. What do you expect?" said Maximillian curtly.

"Oh, there you are, Max," the beauty cooed, looking beyond me. "I was just about to send Hannelore for you. There's something we need to discuss."

"No doubt it concerns another necessity for the Ringstrasse house," he said dryly.

"Of course."

"Well, it can wait. This woman has just arrived from a long journey. It behooves us to see to her comforts first."

"Maximillian," Friedericke said throatily, chin tilted in my direction. "Let's avoid a scene, if we can."

"By all means, Tante," he responded, turning to me. "I shall escort Miss Hopkins myself."

"That's what Hannelore is for," Iris said coolly. "I must talk to you now, Max, before I—"

"Before you what, Iris? Go out for the night?"

"She's only accompanying me to Fralingers'," Friedericke supplied. "Rudolph invited us for a late supper. You know how he is always trying to make a party. The man likes fun."

Maximillian's brows rose at that last word. It was the second time we both heard it this night, and he turned to me instantly. "My apologies, Miss Hopkins. I'll see you to your suite now."

"I'll be gone when you come back, Max. We're already late," announced Iris.

"Go, then, dear. Whatever you want to discuss can wait."

Iris stormed down the hallway, her dainty footsteps echoing sourly on the marble floor.

"Oh, dear, dear me!" exclaimed the dowager, her fingers to her cheek. Then she pivoted smartly to chase after her niece.

Struggling to smother a harsh curse, Maximillian pounded his fist against the wall. A moment later he turned to me, his eyes angry blue flames, his voice subdued. "Again, forgive me." Without another word he led me and the maid in the other direction.

The hall was long and cluttered here, difficult to navigate on this floor. Trunks and tables, chairs and desks, umbrella stands, bird cages, clocks, and jardinieres slowed our way. It looked like a cachement area of some sort, a place where goods were held for safekeeping. There were new, extravagantly designed pieces of furniture, and I thought I would like to examine them more carefully sometime even though they were overly decorated for my taste.

We were soon in a different part of the mansion, I realized. Leaving behind faded walls and dark, dusty cornices, we made a turn to the left and passed a music room, a small library, and a drawing room that was richly appointed. Then Maximillian stopped.

"This will be your suite, Miss Hopkins."

I was amazed. These were not the rooms Sophie had taken me to. They were prettier, more feminine, more elegantly furnished.

"Your bags will be sent up immediately," he added, his composure restored. "Hannelore will assist you in whatever comforts you need at the moment."

"Thank you, Dr. Schaller," I murmured.

"Not at all," he responded, polite and reserved. Then he left.

"If you be wantin' a bath, miss, 'tis through that door. Brand new equipment and never once used." She lowered her voice. "These were Frau Doctor's rooms. All new and now forgotten."

"Iris', you mean?"

"Yes."

"Didn't she like them?" I asked softly.

The girl leaned closer. "She's movin' out." Then with a sheepish, guilty look she pleaded, "Don't say I said so."

When she closed my door, I walked through the rooms, gawking at the furnishings, the elaborate ornamentation. The suite was a showplace. The bed and bureau and dressing table were made of satinwood with decorative inlays and bandings. Gilded mirrors with carvings of birds, foliage, and fruit adorned the walls, as did fancifully ornamented matching girandoles. But the pièce de résistance was the long blue glass placed in the wall that led to the dressing room. In an overlay of opaque white and muted colors, Iris, the mythical goddess of rainbows, was breathtakingly depicted. Dressed in a veil of the sheerest silk, she glided down a rainbow.

Struck by this work of art, I moved slowly on to the bathroom and found it just as impressive. Spacious beyond my imagining, the room featured a long octagonal tub cased in paneled wood. At its head there were several valves offering a variety of choices: douche, plunge, sitz, hot, and cold. This was unheard-of luxury, a one-of-a-kind item that Iris must have had custom-made.

Iris.

I easily pictured her artfully coifed blond tresses, her delicate, foxlike face, and her lovely figure encased in ivory silk. Her eyes were hazel, a strange mosaic of pale gold and gray. They were large eyes, but there was a distant, empty quality to them. Like the woman herself, they looked pretty, but they betrayed a certain falseness. She reminded me of a pearl, this Iris, a beautiful, wooden pearl.

She was married to Maximillian, I reminded myself. But theirs was an unhappy union. I gathered from their fight that they had been estranged for some time, and I wondered what had gone wrong in their marriage. I remembered, too, that Max spoke of a son. He had sounded worried, near desperation, when he mentioned his child. Their child!

As these thoughts tumbled in my mind, I prepared myself for bed. It would do little good to dwell on them. There was no reason to do so. My purpose here did not involve this troubled family. I had traveled hundreds of miles to work with Dr. Demel, to honor my father. There was no reason to get drawn into problems of the household. Best I avoid them.

As I closed my eyes, no inner voice whispered of the difficulties, the foolhardiness, of this intention. No instinct warned me of the evil that lurked so slyly before me, the malice I would be helpless to avoid because of my commitment to vindicate my father.

✝ Chapter Three

The morning dawned clear and cool, the air pure and sweet. From my balcony I had an expansive view of my surroundings, and I saw the beauty of the villa's setting for the first time.

Softly rolling hills flowed into one another to form the long, gentle, endless sweep of forests known as the Viennese Woods, the Wienerwald. My gaze moved down the dark slope below me, across the dewy grass of a meadow that was resplendent with sunshine, and along a stream that fed a pool. The sound of running water floated up, and I closed my eyes to savor the moment.

I remembered walking in the Wienerwald with my father, holding his hand and listening to stories about witches and gnomes. I remembered the boots and loden coat he had bought me for such outings and how he taught me to say *Grüss Gott*, good day, so I would greet other hikers appropriately. It was easy to think back, for these were the good times that made wonderful memories of my childhood.

Of my life eons ago.

Upon opening my eyes, I studied the paths that ran down the slope before me. A squirrel scurried about, collecting food. A man approached the little creature, an elderly man whose posture and drab clothes lent him a sad, even tragic, air. With a wide swing of his cane he chased the poor animal away and gave out a thin, shrill laugh.

My gaze traveled on, sweeping across the pines, then turning down the winding road by which I had arrived the previous night. I stared at that road for reasons I could not quite discern. And I felt, even then, that the road symbolized some kind of boundary, a demarcation, separating what went before in my life with what was to follow.

Shivering, I drew my wrapper closer to me and returned to my room. Within moments there came a knock at the door.

"Don't hurry down, miss," Sophie said, "but when you're ready, breakfast will be waiting."

"I'll be there soon."

"No rush, really."

I looked at my portmanteau for a moment, wondering what I should wear. And when I turned back to the girl to inquire about the rest of my belongings, I saw she had left, disappearing so quickly that there was only a sense of movement by the door, a disturbance of air so slight it was almost mysterious.

Shutting the door, I moved quickly to wash. The luxurious tub would have to wait until someone educated me in its use. I dressed just as fast, wondering at my haste. I could eat when I wanted, at my own leisurely pace. Sophie had said as much, but I felt compelled to go downstairs and look for Dr. Demel because the call to breakfast seemed designed. Somehow I sensed he had sent the maid for me, that her appearance was perhaps a reminder for me to set about my task at his house. If so, my host could have communicated this to me in a more direct fashion. I understood forthrightness. I did not like having to read between the lines. I wasn't used to it.

Dr. Demel was being polite, I chided myself. But later, when I looked back on my first day at this house, I realized that even at this point I was susceptible to his quiet control.

Arranging my hair with care, I gave myself a final glance in the mirror, and descended the stairs.

"Are you the American?" a small voice asked.

"Why, yes, I am," I said, turning to find a young boy behind me. He was tall, slim and had a delicate face with shadows beneath intense blue eyes. There was no doubt whose son this was. He favored his father, Maximillian.

"I'm Emily Hopkins," I said, extending my hand.

"Hello," he replied with a shy, yet speculative look. "I'm Peter."

"I'm going to breakfast." Recalling Maximillian's conversation with Iris about their son's lack of appetite, I decided not to ask him to join me, but to have him direct me to the appropriate room.

"You're almost there," he told me politely.

"Would you like to show me the rest of the way?"

"Yes." To my surprise, he reached for my hand and led me.

He was about seven, unless I missed my guess. His height and maturity indicated this more than any other aspect of size and manner, for the lad appeared sickly and frail, lost in his baggy clothes. He stopped at a room where his father was sipping coffee and reading a newspaper.

"Papa."

Maximillian's eyes lit up at the word. "Peter, how good of you to bring Miss Hopkins. Come in. Both of you. Have some breakfast."

The slim fingers in my hand tensed and slid from my grasp. It was only then that Maximillian noticed where his son's hand had been, and I thought I detected a pleased expression on his face before it changed to a frown when Peter politely declined his offer.

"I've already eaten, Papa."

"Won't you have a little more?"

Peter shook his head.

The air became charged between father and son, and this made me think they had exchanged these words many times previously. Maximillian looked pleadingly, bleakly, at the boy, and finally with a sigh of resignation, he said, "Maybe later."

Before he left, Peter looked at his father with an expression of sad relief, while I, feeling awkward, tried unobtrusively to see what food was offered. Perhaps the lad preferred something else. But the bountiful buffet table, laden with cereals and breads, with butter, honey jams, and platters of sausages and aromatic cold cuts, left little to wish for.

"I hope the selection appeals to you, Miss Hopkins."

"I had no dinner last night, sir. It looks heavenly."

He waved me over. "Why not?"

"Are you inquiring into my eating habits, too?" I spoke teasingly, but the man looked embarrassed.

A smile of self irony tilted the corners of his mouth. "I can't believe I said that. Now, if I promise to be polite, will you join me? I have but a few quiet minutes left before making the rounds of my patients."

Setting my plate down, I told the maid I would like some tea, then I sat opposite this remarkably good-looking man. While I ate, he asked me if I had slept well, if I found my suite comfortable, if everything was to my liking. I was struck by his graciousness, and I thought he was again trying to make up for my terror in the garden the previous night.

Replying affirmatively to all the above, I studied his face, for despite his polite inquiry and my positive reply, I noted little relief or pleasure there. His strong features could not mask what appeared to be a gnawing worry, especially when I mentioned his son.

"Such a fine boy," I said, "the way he introduced himself to me."

"Thank you."

"You must be proud."

"Very."

With such terse comments, I thought it best to drop the subject, but Friedericke, standing in the doorway, chose to prolong it.

"I've said it before, and I'll say it again, Max. What that child needs is a good physic."

"Tante!" my breakfast companion mildly admonished his aunt. "The source of his eating problems is emotional, not physical."

"Then it's a case of the shoemaker's child going shoeless." The plump dowager wagged a jeweled finger. "Take my advice, and the boy will eat like a horse. He'll run around and play again just the way he used to. Poor thing has no energy."

"You don't have to remind me. I'm well aware of it." The abruptness was gone from Maximillian's tone now. A weary bleakness replaced it.

"And don't push him to eat," Friedericke went on. "Ease up for heaven's sake. Nobody likes to be forced to do anything."

"I'll try," Maximillian said. He glanced at his watch and took a last sip of coffee. Standing, he nodded to both of us, then left.

"I hope I didn't overdo it," Friedericke admitted. She took a plate, filled it, and sat next to me. "Reminds me of Iris and her brother, Werner. I never had any of my own, but I know from them that children don't eat well sometimes. It's normal. Maximillian makes all too much out of this, if you ask me."

I thought as much, but did not comment. We began to eat, and after a pause just long enough to be polite, Friedericke turned to me.

"You're here to work with my brother, Dr. Demel?"

"Yes."

"Something involving the clinic?"

"In a way, yes."

"Goodness, I'm impressed. What will you be doing?"

"I hope to visit the patients. You see, I'm trained to help them. But mostly, I'll be writing a biography."

"Whose?" Her voice had risen.

"My father's."

"What a delight," she said. "Now forgive me for asking who he is, but I know precious little about medicine. That's his field, I assume."

I told her of my father and his former connection with Dr. Demel. She listened attentively. And when I mentioned that this was my second trip to Vienna, Friedericke could scarcely contain herself.

"Oh!" she exclaimed. "You could not have returned at a better time. The whole city is agog with wonder and excitement. The Viennese are riding a splendorous crest these days."

Not all the Viennese, I reminded myself, recalling vivid impressions of my own ride from the train station the night before, but I kept the thought to myself. It wasn't hard to do, for I could barely get a word in edgewise. The woman was ebullient.

"New buildings. More elegance. Fancy balls. You'll love it here," she said.

"We'll see," I said simply. A social whirl was hardly my priority in Vienna. Or at home, for that manner.

The dowager seemed deflated. "Tut, tut, all young women love to dance." Her eyes grew dreamy. "To be your age again."

After a moment, she turned to her food and ate quite indelicately, gustily relishing each mouthful. The woman's style was excessive. She seemed to go overboard with everything. Her dress was outlandish. As absurd as the outfit she wore last night. Feathers and furs mixed like a tossed salad on a background of fuchsia and purple. Where was the woman's taste?

"I'd marry nobility."

"Pardon me?" I was woolgathering.

"If I were young," she repeated, "I'd marry . . . oh, bother!" she finished, slathering butter on her pretzel bread and chomping into it.

We ate in companionable silence, each occupied with our thoughts. When I wanted to leave, my parting was somewhat abrupt, but not awkward. The woman seemed pleased to be able to linger alone over her coffee.

Uncertain of the direction of Dr. Demel's study, I attempted to reach the hall first. The handles on three doors did not respond to my touch. I tried a fourth and found myself in a small breakfast nook just off the kitchen. Peter was alone there, looking at the rolls in a baking tin. He touched them gingerly as if testing their warmth. Appearing satisfied, he gave a furtive glance around. Not wanting to frighten him, I stepped back quickly, still curious. When I felt it was safe to observe him again, I leaned closer to the doorjamb and watched him bite into a roll. Given the scene at breakfast with his father, I wondered if Maximillian was pushing the child to eat, and if Peter's selective appetite was a reaction to his father's forcefulness. Maybe Friedericke was right. Yet Maximillian did not seem to be an overbearing father, just a worried one, a man overly sensitive to his child's eating habits. We all have blind spots, I thought. Perhaps this was Maximillian's.

I had now found my way back to the main hallway. "Sophie," I said, "I'm lost. Where is the doctor's study?"

"There, miss." She pointed to a paneled door that was ajar. "Right in there."

I knocked. No answer. I knocked again, daring to peer in. The room was dreary, despite the daylight. Stacks of paper and journals stood in piles, cluttering work space and floor. Unlike other parts of the villa, the room had not been refurbished for years. And a smell, stale and disagreeable, greeted me. At his desk, hand to his forehead, Dr. Demel appeared to be meditating. I knocked a third time. "Dr. Demel," I whispered.

Still no response.

I cleared my throat pointedly and began again. "Professor."

The man turned at once, and I noticed his heavy-lidded eyes and tufted brows. "So it's you, Miss Hopkins. Come in."

It was hardly the response I had expected. "If this is a bad time, I'll return later."

He looked relieved. "Would you mind?"

"No, not at all."

"We can begin tomorrow."

I nodded. "It's up to you."

"Thank you, Miss Hopkins." So saying, my host swung around in his chair and assumed his earlier pose, his body stiff, his mind, I supposed, gathering previous thoughts.

Anxious to leave, I backed my way to the door, bumping clumsily into a stack of books. Dr. Demel turned at my apology and regarded me intently, soberly, as if weighing something. No word came from him, though, not a sound. I could discern no clear expression on his face, only a mingling of emotions forlorn and anxious before he picked up a letter and stared at it, absorbed anew. He was an odd man, living in a strange place, and when I left him to go outside, its peculiarities became even more apparent.

The house was huge, several stories high. Built of tan stucco, its design was baroque. Grand baroque. It seemed to rise out of the ground, one floor above another, in a dizzying flourish of ornamentation. The two wings to the mansion, one for the clinic, the second for the family, had rooms with balconies, and the grillwork on each boasted the same gold *D* I had seen on the entrance gate.

Walking around the house, my gaze was caught by an incongruity on the top floor, for among the perfect series of balconies there appeared to be one missing. On the floor directly below there was no balcony either. But here there was an area of lighter, newer stucco that looked like a patch. It appeared to conceal something as if there had been a mistake, a change of mind, perhaps a wish to hide something. The cover-up was primitively executed as if done in haste, and, as I studied it, I wondered fleetingly if this was the outside wall to the room with no windows. The room with the coffin. It could not be, I told myself, for that small room was on the first floor. These irregularities were curiosities that fueled my imagination.

I walked on.

The grounds were well maintained, but perfunctorily designed. All too similar. There was nothing unique. They appeared mundane to my taste and brought forth no emotion from me. So I had to wonder again if my fanciful imagination, my liking for the unusual, made more out of what I saw in the next terraced area.

This one, a topiary garden, was small but interesting. Again, it was trimmed to sterile perfection, but at least one decorative shape was different from the next. Fish, birds, and beasts from the forest encircled its inner walls, but on each side of the steps that led to the woods there were two shapes opposite one another that I could not quite identify. I looked intently and thought I saw horns and pointed chins. Two devils carved out of boxwood.

A cloud scudding across the sun changed the play of light and shadow here, and, an instant later, the demons vanished. Fascinated by my changing perceptions, I watched once more. And when the cloud mass passed, I again saw twin likenesses of Satan, a step's width apart. Tense. Rigid. Like the house they adorned.

Devils, I thought. *Devil's House,* for that's what I heard the coachman shout. I remembered his shrewd smile and his sardonic laugh. I thought of the moody and mysterious Dr. Demel, the discord in his home, and I worried about what I had come to in Vienna. But my coming had purpose so deeply felt I could let nothing dissuade me.

Down those steps I went. There was not much of a path here and I hesitated briefly, recalling my fright last night. But the chitter of songbirds and a child's laughter drew me. I smiled, my boots crunching the carpet of needles and leaves.

"Miss Hopkins," Peter said, "this is Herman, my duck. He follows me everywhere. See?"

The boy darted from tree to tree, and the duck, with a bit of a swagger, followed him dutifully.

"I'm impressed."

"Want to see where he lives?"

"Of course." What better had I to do? Besides, the child was a delight.

Off we strolled, hand in hand, through the trees, around the stables, and past a fenced paddock. All the while the boy whistled, hummed, and talked to his pet.

"This is it," he said when we reached a small pond. "And these," he said as he pointed to the other ducks paddling around, "are his brothers and sisters and cousins and uncles."

"Quite a family."

And quite a different Peter!

Gone was the sadness I noted earlier. The boy was like any other child I'd known. Even his thin face had color.

Other voices came from some distant path. When I looked toward them, Peter said, "If it's eleven o'clock, that's Papa out with his patients. Every day he takes them for a walk."

"Exercise is good for them."

"That's what Papa says. Helps get their minds off themselves."

The lad spoke easily with a maturity beyond his tender years. I was pleased to hear the pride in his voice. I once had a father I had revered, and I felt the tenuous bond already established with this child grow stronger.

"Tell me, Peter, what else do you do besides play in the woods and take care of Herman?"

"Fish."

"How about school?"

"A tutor comes." He looked somewhat subdued when he said this, and I attributed the choice of a tutor over school to the child's fragile health.

"And after your lessons, you fish?"

"At the brook."

"Is your schoolwork over today?"

He hedged a bit. "Not exactly."

"Well, when it is, maybe we can go fishing."

"Really, Miss Hopkins?"

"Really."

As he scampered off, the voices became clear, and in the next moment I saw Maximillian, two attendants, and a motley group of others walk down the wide path to the house. The doctor greeted his beaming son, then looked up at me and came over.

His long-legged, purposeful strides pushed his starched white laboratory coat open to reveal a rugged, trim, athletic man.

His eyes were alive with delight, and I thought he looked splendid.

"Peter seems beside himself, Miss Hopkins. What did you do?"

"Give him a promise."

His brows rose in surprise. "Of what?"

"A fishing expedition."

"Wonderful," he said, his handsome face spreading in a warm smile.

I wanted to ask him to join us, but thought the gesture so bold and inappropriate I blushed. To cover up my embarrassment, I quickly offered him some stale bread for the ducks. He seemed amused by this, yet I thought I saw a subtle shift in depth in his luminous blue eyes, and I became acutely aware of his undivided attention.

Long moments later he took several bread cubes and scattered them upon the surface of the pond. They were gone in a snap, and when he looked at me again his expression had turned bleak, his voice grave.

"Peter is not well, Miss Hopkins. And I fear he will soon become too weak . . ." He left the painful thought hanging.

Seeing his distress, I told him I would do what I could to encourage the boy's appetite. I did not want to pry, but I felt, since he raised the subject of his son's health, that I could ask some questions about Peter's strange behavior, especially if I were to help him.

I should have known right then that I was treading on treacherous sands. I should have realized I was getting involved in a struggle that was other than my own. But even if I had perceived a warning, some small flag of danger, I don't know if I could have prevented myself from offering help at this time. Peter and his father were engaging people. They caught me up and drew me in like some big ocean wave.

"How long has the boy been like this?"

"For a few months, off and on."

"How much weight has he lost?"

"It's hard to say."

"What do you think is causing his poor appetite?"

The man struggled with his feelings. "For a while I thought it was related to his mother's absence. At least that's what might have triggered it." His gaze became distant. "But sometimes I'm not sure."

I wondered what had gone wrong between Maximillian and his wife. Did they just drift apart, or was there something inherently wrong with their union from the beginning? I wondered if I should tell Maximillian that I saw Peter eating in the kitchen when no one was watching, but decided against it. I did not want to break the fragile trust I was building with the boy. I thought I could better help him if I kept his secret.

"You seem to have established a rapport with him, Miss Hopkins. I can't tell you how appreciative I would be if you would help him."

Hearing the raw concern in his voice, I nodded. "Yes, of course."

"There's something else," he admitted ruefully. "The child has occasional nightmares."

"Oh, poor boy."

"Yes." The man cleared his throat. "And I'm sorry to say your suite is nearest his room."

Maximillian knew this, of course, when he brought me to my chambers last night, but I could not point this out and be polite. Moreover, as I turned the fact over in my mind, I discovered I did not find it so disagreeable. I genuinely liked Peter. What could be the harm?

An awkward silence fell between us. "It's no matter," I finally replied.

The man smiled, regarding me keenly, his expression a mingling of query and approval. "I'm beginning to think you're heaven-sent, Miss Hopkins."

Color flared across my cheeks. "Hardly."

He still studied me, struggling, I thought, with his own self-consciousness. "In any case," he said, regaining his composure, "I'm most appreciative." In an abrupt change of subject, he offered his arm. "Shall I take you back to the house?"

"It's not necessary. I have time to spare, and I like to explore."

"As you wish, Miss Hopkins."

The path sloped downward, cool and shaded. Large mushrooms grew between the gnarled roots of black fir, and the air was rich with the tang of pine and humus. My hope was the path would take me back to the stables and then to the house.

I was wrong.

I found myself getting deeper and deeper into a darkling wood. Shadows pressed in, dense and screening. Shifting restless feet, I told myself to stop thinking about Maximillian and pay attention to my surroundings. My sense of direction was never my forte. This fact and the memory of the rough characters I had met last night made my stomach churn.

Trembling on the brink of uncertainty, I retraced my steps back to the pond. The ducks were gone. The water rippled strangely from the breeze that hissed through the pine branches. I wanted to go back the way I had come with Peter, but I stood indecisively by the edge of the water. Oddly enough, there was little that seemed familiar. Neither the trees nor the bushes. Where were the ducks?

Just then something large and noisy dashed through the woods, scuffling leaves and snapping twigs. Disturbed even more, I turned and saw a tall man behind me with black eyes, and a black curling mustache, with a wreath of cigar smoke above his head.

"Well," he said familiarly, too familiarly, walking toward me. "I'm Werner, and you are . . ."

"Miss Hopkins."

"Should I know you?"

From his name I knew he was Iris' brother. If the communication were normal in this house he would have recognized me, but I shook my head and let matters go at that.

"My, we're pretty," he said, his gaze traveling over me with insulting innuendo.

"Can you direct me to the house?" I asked.

"Going there myself," he answered. "Follow me."

After we walked for a while, I saw Herman toddling toward us, relatives in tow. They were skirting their hutch when Werner took the stub of his cigar and tossed it into the water of the pond that I had been looking for and obviously missed.

Siss. Sisst!

Herman scrabbled toward the sound.

"Don't let him do that," I cried. "He'll choke." I started to run, but my companion laughed and grabbed my arm.

"I'll get it."

He was quick, I admit, producing the offending cigar stub between two fingers. "See, no harm done."

I was silent and began to walk on.

"My, we're touchy, too."

I still said nothing.

"So what are you doing here? At the mansion, I mean."

I told him my story, ending with a rundown of the family members I had met. "Is there anyone else I should be prepared for?" I asked.

He laughed again. "No, you have it right. Just the six of us. My uncle, aunt, my sister Iris, her husband Max, and their son Peter. My father is now deceased, and I've taken over his position at the house."

"What do you do?"

"Keep the books."

I watched him slide his hand inside his breast pocket and lift up something that actually resembled a small book, though it might have been his cigar case. Then, as if thinking better of it, he let the black leather object slip back down into its place.

"You must have a penchant for accuracy."

"I'm a stickler for it, Miss Hopkins."

"So much the better for the sanitarium."

"Indeed."

I felt I had nothing more to say to this man. I did not like the tightness in his expression, his curling smile, or the way he had presumed upon my acquaintance. His manner was most disagreeable, unctuous at times. I was anxious to get back to the house, away from him.

The path grew steeper. Following Werner, I took each step with care, avoiding the many stones and fallen branches before me. At a nearby stream I realized this was a different route than the one Peter and I had taken earlier. Fear prickled down my spine. Then I sensed—heard actually—that my willing guide and I were not alone. When we paused, sounds of twigs snapping came from the other side of the brook.

Werner preceded me across the brook. I had little difficulty crossing it, for large, flat rocks offered an easy access. Still, I watched my footing, unaware of Werner's intent. The last rock was a hop from the bank. I made a quick calculation, took a jump, and landed, to my shock and distaste, in Werner's waiting arms.

At that moment Maximillian and Peter broke through the bushes, stunned at the tableau before them.

"What are you doing, man?" Maximillian roared.

"Keeping an appointment," Werner lied.

My flesh started to creep at the closeness of this vile person, at his insult, and I pulled away.

Werner's mouth curved into a caustic smile, meant more for his brother-in-law than for me. "Jealous, Max? You're a married man. Remember?"

Maximillian's eyes narrowed. He appeared quite confident in his reply. "When I consider the source of that comment I could laugh, Werner. Or should I gag?"

Werner's silk brows jacked up. "My, my, look who is getting riled."

I looked at Peter who was clutching his fishing rod, and I smiled to divert his attention. "Didn't take you long."

"I'm all ready, Miss Hopkins."

"Another time, Peter," Maximillian interjected. "You're going home with me."

Peter tried to smile above his father's reproof. "But—"

"No buts. Come along," Maximillian replied, still ignoring me. Then he took his son's hand and left.

Werner came to my side, thrusting his chin toward the departing pair. "I'm afraid he's a moody man, Miss Hopkins." Though the words were sympathetic, Werner's tone was not, and, when I gave him a sharp look, I saw a smug little smile slide across his face.

I could not wait to go back to my room, to leave behind his nastiness, but I could not walk with Maximillian for he was cold, aloof, an unapproachable stranger now.

I needed to be alone, to sift through my thoughts, gather my wits, calm myself. I needed relief. A bath. The bath. Iris' bath; the thought recurred and became a distracting refrain.

I found the wide path to the house, flew down it, and ran inside. I tried two different passages before happening upon the right one.

My door stood half-open. Why?

With trembling hands I touched the wood, my fingers tickling its panels. I held my breath and pushed, hoping for silence and peace.

But something scraped or scratched now. With every footstep I heard it. Like some haunted creature, I scuttled to the bed. I removed my shoe and laughed hysterically. A piece of paper was stuck to its sole. I had caught a scrap somewhere.

I picked it up. No, it was a message scrawled in minuscule letters.

The horn, the horn, the lusty horn is not a thing to laugh or scorn.

I blinked and reread the statement. Was it meant for me? If so, I could make no sense of it. No sense of anything in this villa. Since my arrival, nothing had been as I had expected. The Demel house was sterile, frozen in a twilight gloom. Its inhabitants were strange and hostile.

I felt pitched into a tempest I did not understand, a maelstrom of dark events that began to mock my self-assurance and fuel my growing fears.

✝ *Chapter*
Four

It was late the next morning when Dr. Demel sent for me. I had already dressed and eaten, and was eager to begin, so I went quickly to his study. He was a different man than the one I saw yesterday. Gone was the worry, the restless reflection. He was businesslike, had few smiles; yet, he was not without a certain discreet charm.

"So prompt, Miss Hopkins. How good of you."

"I'm anxious to start."

"Fine, fine. Me, too. Sit here," he said, motioning to an armchair.

He fussed with some papers, then rifled through a stack of notebooks before finding the one he wanted. "Ah, yes, here it is, Miss Hopkins. I'm ready now, believe it or not."

I smiled.

So did he. But I could not help noticing how the smile dimmed in his eyes before it left the corners of his mouth. I did not know what to make of this strange discrepancy in emotion. It made me feel uncomfortable. "Where do you suggest we begin?" I asked.

"Where all biographers do." He chuckled. "Relax, Miss Hopkins, and your thoughts will come freely. Would you rather I did not take notes for a while?"

"No. But I think I would prefer you to ask specific questions."

"As you wish."

In this fashion the long-awaited attempt to restore my father's reputation began. I related the facts of his birth to a wealthy family in Boston. I related what I could remember of his parents, what I had learned about his youth, his siblings, his formative years and early schooling.

"The Boston years seemed to have been a happy time for your father."

"Definitely. He always had a nostalgia for his childhood and the city."

"How many years did you live there?"

"Let's see." I began to count on my fingers. "Several years at the university and medical school. That would have made him about twenty-five. He stayed there for his post-graduate work—"

"He trained there?"

"In part, yes." It was strange, I thought, that Dr. Demel did not know this. He portrayed himself as my father's close colleague. Professionals who have worked together usually know one another's academic qualifications.

"With whom did he train?"

Again, I was surprised. This time I showed it, and Dr. Demel skillfully steered the conversation forward. Still, I was left with a feeling of unease as I went on somewhat mechanically to answer questions about my mother.

"What was her maiden name?"

"Everett."

"Where did she grow up?"

"Boston."

"They met there?"

"Yes."

"Was her family wealthy?"

"No."

"Did his parents mind?"

"His father, yes. His mother, no."

"Did you like his father?"

"He was a stern man as best I remember."

"Can you give an example of this?"

I hesitated, for I could give many. "If you don't write it down."

"Trust me."

I closed my eyes, recalling one painful event. "I was six. It was my birthday, in fact. I had been led to believe my grandfather was going to give me a doll. He had said as much. He greeted me with a handshake before my party and gave me a very small package. Mystified, I turned it over and over. He asked me if something was wrong. I said no, opening the package hurriedly. My face fell as I gazed at a bar of chocolate. I could not contain my disappointment. Where was the doll? A traitorous tear rolled down my cheek.

" 'What were you expecting, Emily?' the old man asked.

" 'Nothing, Grandpa. I love chocolate.'

" 'It does not appear so,' he said, lifting the bar out of my hand with two long fingers. 'You're an ungrateful child,' he scolded, 'and must learn the hard way.' "

I opened my eyes and found Dr. Demel's penetrating gaze on me. It was not really unkind, but it was more intense, more knowing than sympathetic. I realized I was speaking less of my father's life than of my own. "Most children are sensitive," I said. I sounded defensive.

"Are you still very sensitive?"

I tried to laugh away the question. "Hardly." But, in truth, sometimes I felt I was. I feared I was going to blush. I had to overcome the uneasiness I felt with this man if we were to work together productively.

"You're not good at hiding your feelings. Isn't that right, Miss Hopkins?"

Now I did flush. "Sometimes."

My host had the grace to change the subject. "It's past midday. I won't keep you much longer. You will, no doubt, want to eat and rest for tonight."

I gave him a quizzical look. "Tonight?"

"Why, yes. There is to be a ball this winter to benefit my clinic. The committee planning the event will convene here for dinner tonight. It's the least we can do to show our appreciation."

"I didn't know a thing about it."

"I hope you are coming."

"I'll make every effort," I said, rising.

"You'll enjoy it."

"Yes . . . thank you."

At the door to his study, we said goodbye, and I left wondering about the tardiness of the invitation, about what I should wear. I thought about Dr. Demel and how he seemed to be hearing some facts about my father for the first time—facts he should have known. I was so caught up in these thoughts I did not hear Peter right off.

"Are you angry I didn't fish with you yesterday?" he asked.

"Of course not."

"I had to obey Papa."

"I know."

"Can we go today, Miss Hopkins?"

"First I want to eat." I crouched down to his height. "I don't suppose you'd like to join me?"

He looked away.

"Another time?"

He smiled. "Maybe."

"Give me an hour, and I'll be ready."

"Where should we meet?"

"By Herman's pond."

He was grinning when I left him. I went to my room. Hannelore brought my meal, and while I ate I thought about my wardrobe. I discovered I wanted to go to the dinner. I wanted to look special, be at my best. I was flushed with delight. Max would be there. I was more pleased than I had been all day. For several days.

And Iris?

I felt as if a splash of cold water hit me. How could I think in this dangerous way? What could be ahead but pain and disappointment for all concerned if I pursued these wild thoughts?

I went to my wardrobe and sorted through my clothes. It would, no doubt, be a formal occasion. Philadelphia society took philanthropic events most seriously. And this was Europe. Vienna!

No, the pink satin would not do—not sophisticated enough. The saffron chiffon? Too subdued. I wanted to make an elegant impression. My fingers moved quickly to the other side of the magnificent armoire that held my dresses. Yes, here it was, the floral taffeta print. I took it out just as Hannelore returned for my tray.

"Is there anything else, miss?" she asked.

"Yes, would you see that my gown is pressed?"

"Oh!" she exclaimed. "It's a beauty."

Forgetting the tray, the maid swooped up the taffeta in both arms and left. I changed into a serviceable navy skirt and jacket, and then met Peter.

"Lead the way, young man."

We went down the path to the duck pond, collected Herman, and made our way deeper into the woods to a stream.

"There's a big one," he shouted, pointing into the water.

"Where?" I could see nothing.

"Ooops, he's gone deeper now. Hiding beneath that rock."

"Cagey fish, these trout."

He nodded and cast his line. "But not too smart for me."

A few minutes later I saw the rod bend and Peter, with the point of his tongue at the corner of his mouth, played the fish so skillfully it soon landed on the bank by my feet.

"How's that, Miss Hopkins?"

I applauded. "I can see I'm with no amateur."

"Papa taught me."

"No wonder you're so good," I said.

"I'll tell him you said that."

"No, don't."

"Watch," he said, "I'll do it again."

"What are you using for bait?"

"Flies."

"Your own?" I watched him tie a furry little insect on his line.

"Yes, I make my own."

"Your papa taught you how to do that, too, no doubt."

"Of course."

"Would you mind showing me?"

He glanced up and shook his head, smiling. "No, but we have to do it inside where I have all the supplies to make the bugs." His slim arms moved in a wide arc. I heard a quiet plop and watched the ripples spread across the water's surface.

It was an idyllic place, and the next two hours skittered by. Peter caught three more fish while I chased after Herman to prevent him from plunging into the brook and terrifying the trout.

"Next time you stay home," I scolded.

Herman puckered his bill and shuffled his wide feet.

Peter laughed. Then he told me how he'd come here with his tutor and how the man had lost patience with Herman, too. He told me that they ate the fish they caught.

"Not raw, I hope."

"Oh, no, Miss Hopkins, my tutor made a fire, and we cooked them."

Intrigued, I asked, "When was that?"

"A couple of weeks ago."

So the boy did eat when he wanted to. Deciding not to question him further on this sensitive subject, I tucked this fact in the back of my mind. I was growing closer to him and did not want to jeopardize our new and fragile friendship. It was enough that I had to cut the first of our outings short, I thought, but I was aware of the advancing hour and had little choice.

Back at the house the staff was in a frenzy of preparation. Unusual bouquets of flowers had arrived, beautifully arranged and tied with streamers. Silver services and numerous candelabra and sconces were polished to perfection in the dining room. But nothing compared to the glitter and wonder of the huge mirror-lined ballroom with its crystal chandeliers. It opened to a music room that was hexagonally shaped and totally glassed in. An ensemble was to perform here after dinner, I was told. The piano was rolled to its proper position; music stands were set up. It all looked grand, and I found myself caught up in the excitement.

In my room I had Hannelore explain the intricacies of Iris' extravagant bathtub, and I delighted in its wonders. Holding my dress against me a half-hour later, I paraded before the young girl, and we laughed.

"How will I look?" I asked.

"*Wunderbar!*" She grinned, and I gave her a grateful smile.

I began to wonder why Iris was no longer using these rooms. Her Ringstrasse apartment was unfinished which meant she was living here in the house. But where? And what did she think of my use of her suite? I bit my lip, feeling a shade of discomfort spread over my cheeks.

Nevertheless, while Hannelore put the finishing touches to my hair, I decided to satisfy my growing curiosity. "Where does Frau Schaller stay?"

"Away from the family. Near the other wing. She says she has privacy there."

I could not imagine anything more private or luxurious than what she gave up. I wanted to learn more about her and her relationship with Max. I was about to ask when the door burst open and in she swept, face flushed.

"Where are they, Hannelore?"

"What, Frau Doctor?"

"My emeralds!" Iris cried. "I gave them to you to put away last."

I listened in amazement.

The maid look stricken. "In-in the new safe your husband just bought—"

"Oh, that one. That one," she repeated, her voice rising in consternation. "Why didn't someone tell me, for God's sake? Getting me upset like this just when I'm to be ready." She thrust her arms upward, and out she went in a furious swirl.

"Is she always like this, Hannelore?"

"When she's angry or nervous, which is often lately." Her voice lowered to a whisper. "She and her husband don't get along. Like day and night, those two. I shouldn't be sayin' it, but when she's gone, he's calmer. So's Peter . . . sometimes."

"I heard he doesn't eat."

"Who's to say, miss. The lad eats fine in the kitchen. Always lookin' for somethin', he is."

"He has nightmares, I've been told."

She shook her head. "Ach, poor boy. It's different than the way it used to be here. My mother was the maid for the family years ago. She told me the place was full of life."

I found myself wanting to know more, but decided not to ask, for fear of looking too inquisitive. "Well, there's plenty of excitement tonight," I said.

"Of the good kind, miss. Now put your right arm through first," she said, lifting the taffeta. The dress swished to the floor, and when she'd finished buttoning it, she brought her hands to her cheeks. "Oh, my!" she exclaimed. "You're a picture."

I was not sure about that, but I knew I liked the way I felt in this dress. It fitted beautifully, and I was fond of the rose and olive in its floral print. "That's nice to hear," I replied.

" 'Tis true," she said, eyeing me carefully. With a knowing look she added, "Your stay will be very interestin'. Might even liven things up."

"With the good kind of excitement, I hope."

She responded with an unreadable smile.

Dinner was everything I expected: formal, proper, elegant. The five adult members of the Demel family and I were joined by four couples. They all knew each other well, I had been led to believe, yet during the early part of the meal they spoke to one another with careful, even stiff courtesy. It was only after the consomme—when the second wine was served—that their reserve appeared to thaw. To my secret delight I had been seated next to Maximillian, and his discreet asides to me amid the growing chatter around us offered considerable enlightenment.

"Isn't it marvelous," Frau Schleyer intoned breathlessly, "that the Demel family will host this gala evening that we are planning? Everybody who is somebody will take notice."

"Imagine the write-ups in the society columns," another soprano trilled. "We would do well to make it an annual event."

"Splendid," someone else chimed in.

Maximillian turned to me. "A self-serving motive if ever I've heard one. Not a thought given to how the benefit will help the suffering patients, only how it might heighten the status of these rich—"

"Speak up, Max," Werner suggested briskly from his end of the table. "We can't hear you down here."

Maximillian cleared his throat. "I was merely telling Miss Hopkins that the amount of publicity boggles the mind." He smiled silkily at his brother-in-law. "Does it not?"

"Success by dint of your efforts," Dr. Demel was saying, his glass high, his gaze including all guests. "Thank you. I toast you. *Prosit!*"

"Prosit," they cheerfully replied, raising their stemware and looking left and then right.

One voice bubbled over the clinking and laughter. "It will be our second party this season. At the opening of the Burgtheater we'll have our first." Iris was gloriously triumphant.

Friedericke beamed her approval above a double portion of food.

"If it ever opens," a small man piped up.

"Really, Rudolph," his wife chided.

"I mean it. They've been working on it for fourteen years!"

"Thank heavens," said Iris. "Otherwise I wouldn't be able to give a party for its opening." She pouted prettily at the gentleman on her left, and I saw him squeeze her hand.

"In part, it's because of Klimt," Herr Rudolph Fralinger continued. "He caused the delay."

Gustav Klimt was the chief artist hired by the Hapsburgs to paint the ceiling of the theater. He was to depict important milestones in the development of drama from its beginnings to this new theater, which, it was thought, would raise the dramatic arts to a new level. I had read that his original representations for *The Chariot of Thespis* were so radical the artist was stopped by the government.

"Anyone who can lie on a scaffold month after month like Michelangelo and create a work of art deserves credit," said Max.

"Depends what they paint," Werner added.

"The man has no morals," Frau Gudron Weber sniffed. "It's a wonder he kept his job."

"Were the sketches of two women kissing *that* indelicate?" asked Dr. Demel. "They were curved like flowers, I was told."

A shocked hush descended upon the dining room.

Friedericke caught her brother's attention and rolled her eyes heavenward.

I felt Maximillian's knee nudge mine ever so slightly beneath the table. I turned to him, and he returned my glance, a smile twitching his lips.

When I looked up, I saw Dr. Demel watching me through lazy-lidded eyes. No smile touched his mouth.

There were only the sounds of eating. Though everyone appeared to enjoy the feast during this relative quiet, Iris must have felt that the lull in conversation stretched uncomfortably.

"The work of Klimt aside," she said, retrieving the discussion, "no city can compare to ours."

"I think we must include him when we speak of the creativity of the Viennese," Max responded. "He'll go far. He is ahead of the rest of the art world right now."

"Time will tell," Friedericke said, trying to keep the exchange between husband and wife neutral. "Meanwhile, let's salute our Vienna, the city of genius composers, artists, and philosophers."

There was another round of toasts.

"To Mozart."

"Strauss."

"To them all."

"And to the Viennese who foster their achievements."

"Foster? We *exalt* in them."

"Prosit!"

The footmen served still another wine, this one to accompany a galantine of pheasant that was filled with a savory oyster and sage dressing. The food was aromatic, delicious, and beautifully arranged.

"And with this exquisite vintage we welcome our guest from America," I heard Dr. Demel say.

The crystal was raised again.

"How long will you stay?" Frau Weber asked.

I was not sure. I turned to my host.

"Until our work is finished," he said, eyeing me steadily in his penetrating way. "However long it takes."

I felt vaguely uneasy at this response. Why did I not trust the man? He was doing something wonderful for my father. For me, too.

"Well," Frau Weber added, "the ball season starts on January sixth and goes all month. One ball after another."

"We call it *Fasching,* Carnival," said Iris for my benefit. "And the Industrialists' Ball is an absolute must. Its tickets are the most expensive."

As the conversation continued, I began to grasp the seriousness with which these Viennese valued their pleasure and status.

"Remember the ball called the Fourth Dimension?" Iris went on. "Nothing there even vaguely resembled reality."

"Including behavior," Max said under his breath. In words I could barely hear, he added, "I couldn't take it and had to leave."

The guests talked of the benefit they were organizing. It was some months away but required considerable planning.

"You'll still be here, Miss Hopkins?"

"Undoubtedly."

"She'll be a most welcome addition to the festivities," Herr Fralinger noted.

Not until after dessert did the conversation dwindle again. The butler entered and solemnly announced the evening's musical program. We filed into the ballroom two by two. Maximillian walked with his wife, and Werner escorted me.

"Do you like Mozart?" he asked.

"Does anyone not?"

"What do you like about him?"

"His music has depth, and sometimes a playful, whimsical quality. It's almost as if he is teasing his audience."

"Interesting, Miss Hopkins. I never thought of his appeal in quite that way. You'll enjoy the performance, I'm sure."

I did in spite of the fact that I sat between Werner and an empty chair. Several movements from one of the composer's piano concertos were sublimely rendered. Almost without realizing it, my eyelashes quietly fluttered down, and I gave myself to the music which filled the mirrored room with wonder.

At the enthusiastic applause, I opened my eyes and could not help but notice Iris' subdued response. She and Maximillian sat in front of me and in seats closest to the aisle. While everyone else smiled, she remained serious and looked down at the hem of her dress, or shoe, as if there was some irregularity there. She whispered something to her husband while my attention was again brought to the performers.

A violinist plucked a string, bent a careful ear to his instrument and struck his bow upon it. Several gas lamps were turned down, and in this diminished light a hush descended. I sensed a movement, a swish of skirts to my right, but closed my mind and eyes to it.

Strains of a rapturous waltz flowed through the room, now with a touch of melancholy, now with sparkling grandness. It was enchantment beyond description, and its intoxicating effect filled my senses.

I felt transported from Demel house. Safe. Away from my fears. I let myself float with this music, let myself relax and dream. . . .

I did not know exactly when the empty chair next to me became occupied, but I knew without looking that Maximillian sat beside me. There was no mistaking the bold shoulder that grazed mine as it had during dinner, nor the clean, manly scent. Caught up in the majestic sweeps of Strauss, I enjoyed beauty and peace: the gifts of music. And I knew with all my heart Maximillian shared them with me.

The applause went on unabated. There were cheers, suggestions to dance, all manner of approval. But not from Iris. The woman was gone.

"Did you ever hear such a rendition?" Werner asked.

"No, I was enthralled."

"We'll have to have these fellows again."

"Haven't they played here before?"

"No. Friedericke recently heard of them. Look at her, she's beaming."

While I watched his aunt speak to the musicians, Maximillian left his chair to join them. It was silly, but I felt let down.

"Something wrong?" asked Werner.

"Nothing." I replied fervently, too fervently, for Werner gave me a quizzical look. Then he saw the direction of my glance and added, "You would do wise, Miss Hopkins, to mind what is yours to mind."

I flushed to the roots of my hair and became immediately grateful to Dr. Demel who was gesturing to me above the heads of his guests.

I heard delighted chatter as I made my way to him.

"Friedericke has started a new trend with this ensemble," Frau Weber mused. "Leave it to her."

"Indeed," Frau Fralinger affirmed.

I think everyone in the family was especially pleased with the evening. It was only later when I was climbing the stairs that I realized how important the success of the evening was to the Demels.

"Your presence was an asset," Werner told me, in an effort to smooth over our earlier conversation.

"That's kind of you," I demurred.

"Think as you wish, but I know we presented ourselves well tonight."

"Is that so important among friends?" I asked.

"These people are more than friends. They're much-needed benefactors." He turned on the step and touched his breast pocket. "My cigars," he said. "Can't go the night without one. I saw you on your way up and . . ." He came closer, his eyes leveling on mine. "You have an effect on me, Miss Hopkins . . . a most decided effect."

I stepped back a pace.

The man laughed and walked on.

Not until I reached the end of the hallway was I able to forget the echo of his laugh. I had, by now, passed the turn-off to my room. I continued on, taking an ell in the passage. I knew it led to the clinic proper. I had never been there. I had no reason to go now, yet on I went through the cluttered corridor, past the stored tables and trunks, the brand new jardiniere, candelabras, and bird cages. They were intricate, gilded, fascinating. They would go to the Ringstrasse house, I guessed.

I must have jarred a container. I heard a muffled gong which startled me. Why? It could only have come from . . . a clock.

Did it?

My curiosity getting the better of me, I decided to take a look and moved forward toward several boxes. What if someone saw me? What would I say?

Go back, a voice within me cried. *Go back.*

But I was already working at the strap on a box. It looked like a bonnet box, but it was deeper. And heavier, I decided, shifting it slightly. I undid the buckle and freed the strap. My fingers moved quickly over the enamel cloth and under the lid. There were shreddings, padding, then something firm beneath. It was cool to the touch. Hard.

Again I heard that deadened tone.

Nervously now, I removed the protective covering. I half smiled. What lay in my hands was an unusual mechanical piece under a glass shade. The bell-shaped glass resembled a vaulted ceiling above a mirrored room. Three couples with their backs to me were elegantly dressed: the women wore crimson and gold velvet detailed with ribbons and lace; the men were in black silk. Without realizing, I must have moved the small lever. I heard a gong, the first few notes of Strauss, and watched the figures turn toward one another.

I gasped and nearly dropped the dreadful novelty out of shock, for within this crystal dome wizened monkeys with sinister smiles mocked me. Their eyes took on a feral gleam as the music commenced. And then, to my stirring horror, the flowing strains of the waltz turned sour. The violins screeched. Still, these creatures danced.

The piece was an affront to good taste, a mockery of the earlier beauty of the evening in the ballroom downstairs. Was it a replica of that room? I turned the music off and noticed, as I did, carved letters in the wooden base. *Death Waltz.* With shaking fingers I covered the glass bell and placed the horrid piece back in its box.

I did not return immediately to my room. I should have, but something urged me toward the clinic. Slowly making my way, my thoughts in a jumble, I wandered down the passage.

At the sound of laughter, I paused. I had no business here. I turned to go. Then I noticed a crack of light beneath a nearby door. I lingered a moment longer—long enough to hear a male voice.

"You slipped away."

"Of course."

"What excuse this time?"

"My dress was badly stained." The woman laughed. "I needed to change."

"He believed it?" the man asked.

A throaty little purr was the reply.

"My clever witch."

Iris, I thought, walking quickly away. I did not recognize the male voice. But I knew visiting hours were long since over, and my heart sank at the sad realization that he had to be a patient.

This discovery took the last bit of pleasure out of the evening. I had no recollection of passing the stored furniture and boxes, or of arriving in the family wing. And when I saw Maximillian there, I felt myself stiffen.

He was smiling at me, walking toward me, humming. "Did you enjoy yourself this evening?"

"It was wonderful." Did I sound convincing?

Max raised his eyebrows. "Yes." He paused and looked at me curiously. "Are you feeling well, Miss Hopkins?"

"Quite."

"You seem a little strained."

"It's nothing. Nothing a good rest can't cure."

"Well, I won't keep you." He chuckled. "I shouldn't detain myself. One or two patients to check on, then I'll turn in."

My God! He'll find her!

I took a step forward, blocking his way. Puzzled again, he studied me, his face touched with surprise. "Miss Hopkins," he said with a note of concern.

With every fiber of my being I became aware of the man, alive to the softness of his voice, the breadth of his shoulders, the blue of his eyes. I glanced downward, but I did not move. I could not. He would be so hurt.

"Miss Hopkins," he said in that soothing way.

What was he thinking? I must appear to him exactly like his promiscuous wife, yet I wanted to protect him from her. But how could I say this? I stepped back slowly, reluctantly, then dashed toward my door.

"Wait," he called.

I turned to find him regarding me somberly.

A long moment passed.

"Good night," I said quietly.

He nodded. "Good night."

Alone behind my door, I felt desperately sad, unable to decide if I felt sorrier for the betrayed patient . . . or the betrayed spouse.

✝ Chapter Five

In the next two weeks a satisfactory routine evolved. I spent the mornings with Dr. Demel, the afternoons at my leisure. My host and I inched our way through my father's life, using the question-and-answer format previously established. I realized again that Dr. Demel seemed as interested in my life as he was in my father's. I could not tell if I was overreacting to the man, for in his presence I felt I had little objectivity.

"Tell me more about your father's upbringing," he urged.

"Which aspect of it?"

"Was he religious?"

"Yes. In the best possible way."

"How do you mean?"

"He taught by example, not by preaching. He was a God-fearing man, but not all caught up in divine retribution the way his father was."

Demel put up a hand. "A moment, Miss Hopkins. This is most interesting. Let me find something to write with."

I waited while he rummaged through his desk. When he triumphantly produced a pen, I continued. "My grandfather was the son of a New England minister who was, according to his family, a man of intimidating rectitude. Adopting his own parents' stern forbidding manner, my grandfather was an avid Bible reader who went about quoting scriptures in an effort to mold our character. He lived with us, and I remember the time when he caught one of the servants telling a lie, how I thought the Lord's vengeance would come down upon the whole household."

"What was the lie about?"

"I don't know. But I remember thinking that he saw this as an opportunity to teach a lesson and he seized upon it with relish."

"What did he do?"

"He ranted on about the fires of hell."

"And how did your father react to this?"

"When the fury abated, he took me aside and said that Grandfather sometimes liked to dwell on the failings of others. He needed to do it, my father thought, because in a way it made Grandpa feel better about himself. By pointing to someone else's wrongdoings, the man could feel satisfied that he was not bad. *He* didn't do such things. *He* was good. That's the way my father explained it."

"Did you really understand this?"

"Not completely at the time. Later, as an adult, I thought that when my grandfather acted like this he probably was protecting himself from his own inclinations. By criticizing others, perhaps he could ignore his own baser instincts."

Demel grew thoughtful. "You're very perceptive, Miss Hopkins. Far more than most."

"I come by my perception honestly, Dr. Demel."

He smiled. "A trait of your father's, no doubt."

I smiled my agreement. "There's something else I remember about this incident of the lie."

"What's that?"

"After the servant was dismissed, my father said simply to me, 'Lies have short legs, Emily. They don't get you very far.' I've never forgotten that."

Dr. Demel laughed out loud, and I joined him.

Looking back on that time of my life was a pleasure beyond description. The warmth and love of my parents, the snug security they provided filled my memory. I was the daughter of a physician, a prominent doctor whose patients' well-being was foremost in his life. My mother never complained about this. She was good-natured, accepting, proud of my father, and taught me to be the same. She always wanted his home to be a haven for him.

We tried to make it that. It was clean, neat, beautifully furnished and comfortable. Even the most formal room was welcoming. I attributed this to the gentleness of my mother's personality, to her poise and quiet assurance which pervaded the house, giving it dignity and warmth. My father was grateful and generous in return.

We liked that, Mother and I, especially when we went out to shop. I remember buying a favorite outfit. It was a red plaid coat with beaver trim, and it came with a matching muff and hat. I remember the saleslady fluttering around me. "She's right out of fairyland, Mrs. Hopkins. Does the doctor proud."

My mother beamed at this. Then, on the way home, she squeezed my hand and smiled. "Our life *is* like a fairy tale, Emily," she said. "We're blessed to have so much. Don't ever forget it, darling."

How could I? How could I forget the cozy fire and tasty cakes that waited for us on chilly days, or the refreshing juices we enjoyed on humid ones. I told Dr. Demel all this, but I do not think he comprehended the full measure of my feelings.

This puzzled me.

Nevertheless, I went on about our family outings: the rides in the park, the children's theater, the ice cream parlors we frequented, and the goodies we always returned with. In the homebound carriage I would sit between my parents, holding my father's hand, leaning on my mother, nuzzling the fur of her coat until I fell asleep. I spoke of these things with wistful yearning. I wanted to linger on them, for I knew the pain I had yet to tell, and I wanted to postpone it.

Dr. Demel must have been aware of this.

"We seem to be going over the same material, Miss Hopkins."

"But detail enriches a biography. The more you know about my father's life, the more interesting an account you can give."

"I realize that, but you're telling me the same thing, that he gave you a life of privilege, only you're saying it in different ways."

"That's not all I'm saying." I was indignant.

He cleared his throat. "Yes, of course."

In the silence that followed, I grew uncomfortable. I disliked the manner in which he regarded me, did not like the shift in his eyes from amusement to something else I could not quite name.

He arched one heavy brow, and I went on. "Such was our happiness until . . . the day my wonderful mother died."

"How did it happen?"

"Childbirth. I was thrilled to learn there would be a baby in the family. Father, too, was beside himself with delight. The pregnancy was a surprise, actually. Apparently my parents had wanted another child for some time, but my mother never conceived. Then, when it happened, the whole household soon knew, and the servants shared in our joy. They doted on my mother and me as never before, making her rest and flattering me about my exalted place as the big sister."

" 'Yer'll be a big help to yer ma if ya sing to the wee one like that,' I remember our maid once saying to me.

" 'But, Mrs. Reilly, I have such a small voice.'

" 'Yer've got the making of a crooner, me darlin'.' "

I paused in my story.

"During the pregnancy I thought everything would be better than before, Dr. Demel. With childlike exuberance I helped prepare the nursery. As time went on and my mother's confinement drew near, the excitement in the house grew. When my mother's time came, I set my little table with my tea service. One place for me, another for the baby. Then I waited."

I stopped again, unable to go on. When I finally could, my voice was lower, strained.

"The tea grew cold. I never touched it. My father came. He looked frightful. I wondered what was wrong. He held me tight. He wept. 'We lost her, Emily. We've lost her and the baby,' he cried."

I was silent once more. I could hear the acorn clock on Dr. Demel's desk ticking. The seconds seemed long in passing. Time. Time. The healer had been time.

"I am so sorry," Dr. Demel said.

Seeing my discomfort, he tried to move my story along. "How did this affect your relationship with your father?"

"We became closer. We spent almost every moment he was not with a patient together. That's how we dealt with our grief. I think I became quite dependent on him."

"What do you mean?"

"I didn't want to go to school."

"How did he react to that?"

"He kept me home."

Demel was surprised. "He did?"

"Yes. He had tutors come to the house."

"How long did this last?"

"Two years."

"How old were you then?"

"Nine."

"When you started with the tutors?"

"No. Miss Perry came when I was seven—when my mother died. I went to school at nine."

"To get back to your father . . . tell me about him after his loss."

"He was devastated, and I think I was a great comfort to him."

"How so?"

"He made a point of eating almost every meal with me. He arranged for my piano lessons and he accompanied me on his violin. He was an American history buff. He read to me, then made me read to him. We went to church together. He supervised my homework, especially my history and science lessons."

"That would seem natural."

"Yes. He told me I had an aptitude for it. He taught me to fish, and when we came home with a stringer full, we always saved one poor thing to dissect. He pointed out its organs. Told me what they did. He even began to encourage me to use his stethoscope and listen to my own heartbeat."

"He was an attentive father."

"A superb father."

"Would you argue that at this time you were all he had?"

"On a personal level, yes. Professionally, no."

"What of his practice, then?"

"I don't understand."

"Did it suffer at all during his grief?"

"Not that I know of. Remember, I was young. But he told me later that after Mama died he started to pay more attention to people's emotions and how they might influence their illnesses. Once a week he began to visit the most progressive asylum in Philadelphia. His medical interests were shifting slightly. He wanted to come to Europe for further study as other colleagues did. He thought of going to France, but he came here to Vienna for a sabbatical instead . . . as you well know."

I observed Dr. Demel carefully when I said this. I watched his response, and I thought I detected an uneasiness in his expression just before he smiled. I didn't know what to make of this. It was strange that he would react this way when he had invited my father here ten years ago, and when he invited me here now to review, among other things, that aspect of Papa's life. It was almost as though I had said something that surprised my host. But what could it be?

I thought back to my own sense of unfamiliarity when I arrived in Vienna and at Demel's house. I remembered my discomfort when I spoke with him earlier about my father's training. Demel seemed to know little about the man who had worked with him.

But Demel was never one to be at odds for long. He quickly regained the initiative.

"We have all lost loved ones," he said. "At one time or another we are bereaved. It's part of life."

Dredging up painful memories was beginning to take its toll on me. I fought back tears.

"There's no avoiding grief," he went on. "No going around it."

I shook my head, not trusting myself to speak.

"Poor child, losing both parents long before you should have . . . and so unexpectedly, too."

I could not look up.

I sensed the man had shifted his weight. He must have leaned forward, for in the next moment I realized he was closer to me. He put his hand on my arm, the diamond in his pinkie ring winking wildly. His palm was damp, and I wished to shake it off.

I met his eyes slowly.

There was something very wrong about the way he was studying me, and I was greatly relieved when he said, "That's all for today, Miss Hopkins."

I composed myself quickly in the hall. It was bad enough that I had let my emotions show in front of Dr. Demel. He, at least, knew the reason for them, but no one else would.

It was natural to hurt when old wounds were reopened. And I suddenly knew I would have to pay a dear price to examine my father's life and ultimately clear his name.

I was growing curious as to how Demel would piece my father's life together. Would he adhere to the chronology of events? Or would he take a more artful approach to his task?

It came to me with some force then, that a biographer had enormous power. He could slant facts, misrepresent events, falsely portray a person. Betray him. And my breath caught when I thought that the account of my father's life was in the hands of someone I was not sure of.

I was rounding the corner, heading for the staircase, when I heard the voices of Iris and Frau Schleyer coming from the small drawing room to my left.

"You'll get us two tickets, then?" Frau Schleyer said.

"Of course," Iris replied.

"*Everyone* is going."

"I knew I could count on you."

"Not to worry. It's as good as done."

"Oh, thank you. Thank you," Frau Schleyer replied. Clasping her hands to her bosom, she closed her eyes. "What a relief."

She sailed past me, ignoring me on her way out of the house. I stepped back, repelled by the cloying scent of gardenias she trailed in her wake. Another door open and out came Friedericke.

"Sarah Bernhardt is sold out opening night, darling. How will you ever get tickets for the Schleyers?"

"I have no intention to."

"But you said—"

"I did it to keep her quiet. She's been begging me for days. It got to be annoying."

"Well, I think I might be able to pull a string or two to help her. After all, she does support the sanitarium."

Iris smiled silkily. "Don't bother, Tante, she's a social nothing. I wouldn't want anyone who matters to think we helped her. It would put *us* in a bad light."

Friedericke reflected on that. "You have a point there."

I could scarcely believe my ears. Iris lied outright to a friend. She dined with the Schleyers and traveled with them. They helped plan the benefit for the sanitarium. Her lofty lifestyle was due in part to their generosity. Yet she would deceive them. And in front of me! As if I were air, she revealed her true feelings. Not because she trusted me; I had no illusion of that. More than likely she considered me of no consequence either. I was stunned at her rudeness. She who sat so primly and made a point of appearing so well-mannered.

In continued amazement I watched as her long fingers slipped into her pocket and withdrew something she held up triumphantly. With a flick of her thumb she produced a fan of green slips.

Friedericke gasped. "Tickets! Extras?"

Her niece nodded.

"Where did you get them?"

Iris smiled secretly. "A friend, shall we say."

"Really, dear, you are most creative. But what will you say to the Schleyers?"

Iris' lip curled higher, exposing her large teeth. "I'll blame the head of the ticket office. I'll say he promised me, then did not come through."

Friedericke looked at me as if noticing me for the first time. She appeared doubtful. "I don't know, dear. Well . . . it's Else Schleyer's birthday next week. You can make it up to her."

"Why bother?" Seeing her aunt's quick glance my way, Iris amended. "I have fittings all week. Buy something for me to give her."

"Such as?"

"Anything . . . as long as it's cheap. My dresses cost a fortune, and Maximillian only allows me—"

"I give you plenty for clothes and gifts." Maximillian had come up behind me.

He stalked forward, snatched the tickets from his shocked wife, and said: "Never mind, I'll buy her present."

"Give back those tickets you . . . ox."

"Not a chance," said Max, holding them higher.

Iris flushed. "I need them."

"Why? We already have our seats."

"Maximillian, please." She tried cajoling him. "Let's not cause a scene."

"*Us?*" he said sarcastically. "You must be joking."

"For heaven's sake, can't we act human this once?"

"Is that the way you're treating Else Schleyer? She's supposed to be a friend. Didn't she find out the name of Barbara Hoffmann's seamstress for you? And didn't you go up the social scale a few points once you could brag that *she* made your clothes? What's fair is fair, Iris. Do something nice for the woman."

"If I had to please everyone who asked me for favors, I'd have no time for anything else."

"You mean you'd have less time to pursue your own affairs."

Iris was silent.

Her husband went on. "You have two sets of rules. One for the way you want to be treated, another for the way you treat others."

"You're way off the mark, Max. I don't make up the rules. I take them as they are. I act in a way that is expected of me."

"By whom? The socially fit?"

"Yes, dammit!" She continued coolly, "Besides, I enjoy it. I like being looked up to."

"And looking down on others. Admit it, Iris, that's what you and your clique do. Your values are skewed." He fingered the tickets. "What scheme do you have for these? Is there some favor you're bargaining for? Someone higher up the ladder you want to impress? Who, dear wife? I'm curious to know."

Iris laughed dryly. "Don't you know, you dumb ox, that everyone can't be a member of our circle? We have to keep the numbers down. Otherwise the group would lose all meaning."

"And well it should. The pecking order among the *Quality* puts the chickens to shame." He smiled derisively. "No, I take that back. Those animals can't reason. You and your elitist friends can. If only you'd look beyond your own noses and see the misery that exists, you perhaps wouldn't be frivolous with money."

"We shouldn't be blamed for the families we were born into. We're educated, refined, and cultured. They're not."

"Many of you are newly rich. Where you go and what you do is all for show. It's enough to make me ill."

Iris moved closer to her husband. Her voice was caustic. "If that's the case, first give me those tickets and then get sick."

She reached up, trying to snatch them from Max's hand, but he moved away, laughing, thwarting her efforts. Iris glared at him, saying nothing. Then she stormed off and slammed a door.

I stood at the threshold, transfixed. It was only then I realized that Friedericke had left. I was alone with Max.

He plowed a hand through his hair. "Forgive me, Miss Hopkins. I was out of control. I didn't mean to get so carried away."

I nodded. He left. I climbed the stairs, thinking again of his disastrous marriage. He and Iris were like oil and water—unable to mix. I had never witnessed such undisguised hate. My parents had had disagreements, but nothing that resembled these bouts. I was embarrassed, shaken. And if I, an adult, could react so emotionally to their fights, poor Peter must be terrified by them.

Is that why he didn't eat? Children often showed their anxiety through stomach distress. How many times did my father treat my tummy-aches after my mother died? A loveless marriage was like a death for a child.

For the parents, too.

No wonder Iris was moving out. No wonder Maximillian let her go. Would they live apart, each having affairs? Iris had already gone that route.

Had Max?

The thought distressed me.

I had not quite reached my room when Hannelore came to tell me that a package had arrived for me.

"It's downstairs. I'll send it up," she said. Surprisingly, she didn't descend the stairs. She followed me inside my room.

"Did you hear that fight?" she asked.

I couldn't deny it. "Yes."

"They're getting worse, those two. If Frau Doctor doesn't move out soon, there's no telling what can happen. She and her husband have tempers. Bad ones."

"I've never witnessed anything like it," I said. "They argue often, you say?"

"Somethin' fierce these last few years." The girl paused, went to my door and closed it. "I suspect you're the quiet type, if you get my meanin', so I'll tell you. My mother worked at this house before me. I grew up hearin' stories about the place. It's different here now, and Mama says it all started after Professor Doctor Demel lost his wife."

I don't know what I expected to hear. Certainly not that. "I never thought the man was married. He didn't appear the type."

"Poor man. He was so good to her . . . even before she took ill. He gave her jewels and furs. A beautiful home. What every woman wants. Course she was young, mind you, nearly twenty years younger than him. And pretty. A shame she passed away."

"How did she die?"

"The strangest thing, it was. She was healthy one month and gone the next. Started with a stomach upset. She thought somethin' at dinner didn't agree with her. But she kept gettin' sick, no matter what she ate and what she didn't. Awful bouts, she had. Then one day she couldn't breathe, and the next thing we knew she was gone."

"So fast?"

Hannelore nodded. "He was all broken up over it."

"What did you think it was from?"

"They traveled a lot and Dr. Demel thinks she picked up a parasite in the islands 'cause she got sick soon after returning from one of them. Always went to exotic spots, they did."

"They were a close couple?"

"My, yes. Nothin' like the Schallers. Frau Demel did everythin' with her husband. Wherever he went, she went. Whatever he wanted, she wanted. The asylum, too."

"You were working here then?"

"Oh, no. I was too young. My ma was here, though."

"How long ago was this?"

"Ten, twelve years ago." The maid sighed. "A pity, I tell you. They had everything. Even lots of money. Course, she brought that into the marriage."

The maid paused, unsure for just a moment.

Her voice lowered. "Some say Dr. Demel got cheated out of an inheritance when she died."

"She didn't leave it to him? Sounds odd if they got along so well."

"There was a big legal mess, I'm told. He got somethin', though."

"Since she was young, maybe the stocks and property, or whatever her family had, were not all in her name."

"I don't know the ins and outs of it." Her voice went lower yet. "My ma says money is tighter around here now than ever."

"Well, don't forget the family is building a new home on the Ringstrasse."

"Who knows." She was suddenly noncommittal. "I'm only tellin' you what I hear, and I hope I haven't said too much." There was a warning in her eyes. "You won't be quotin' me, will you? The Demels don't like us to talk."

"I'm very discreet," I assured her.

For the rest of the day I couldn't stop thinking about this conversation. The more I thought about it, the more I saw Dr. Demel in a different light. He had been married to someone young. Why did I find that difficult to believe? He was a widower. He understood my pain. But when he expressed his sympathy, I thought he tried to establish a rapport with me that I found distasteful.

Hannelore mentioned financial problems. It was hard to believe they existed. No one seemed to want for a thing here, least of all Iris. Did her excesses cause a strain? On the surface, one wouldn't think so. But the new house had to cost a fortune, and maybe its expenses came at a time when the census in the asylum was low.

The sanitarium.

Strange I had not been invited to visit it yet. If my host was eager to learn of its sister institutions in America and of the way they were run, surely he would have given me a tour by now. My father described the organization of these hospitals in detail in his journal. But I had not progressed to this part of his life in my sessions with Dr. Demel.

Hannelore spoke so well of him. It surprised me. Perhaps my assessments of the man were wrong.

These thoughts churned in my tired mind even when I went to bed. I fell asleep quickly, but it was a fitful, troubled rest.

Cruel memories of Papa's enemies tracked me. Like hounds of hell, they came, running me down to a dark world that was filled with pain and horror.

"People won't forgive. They never forget," a voice barked.

"You're good as marked," another sneered.

"No! My father was a good man. An honest one."

"They'll always remember."

Smiles mocked me—demented smiles that widened and pulsed with brutal glee.

"There's no place for you here now."

"Disgraced . . . dismissed."

"No!" I shouted.

The faces pressed down upon me. "Then save yourself. Tell him you're against him."

"Never."

"We will tell him."

"Don't. It's a lie. They're all lies."

I went to Papa's bedroom. "Papa, they lied. Wake up, they lied." Terrified, I lifted his rolling head, his lifeless limbs. I saw the evidence of opiates on his nightstand. . . . "Papa! Papa!" I screamed long and loud.

I bolted up, hurled from the depths of a pit that was dark with terror and pain. My heart was hammering. I was trembling with fear.

"Papa . . . Papa . . ."

The shriek in the night came from another.

"Come, Papa."

From somewhere nearby the cry came again. I listened.

"Papa."

Peter. Of course. Who else could it be?

Grabbing my dressing gown, I opened my door. The corridor was dark, save for a scant thread of light at its far end. I moved toward it swiftly, donning my wrapper.

The door to the last room was opened a crack. I rushed inside. A lamp revealed the boy, flailing under the helpless gaze of the wooden soldier that stood above his bed.

"Peter," I whispered. "It's me, Emily."

Still asleep, he didn't hear me.

"It's all right, Peter. I'm here now." I touched him, and he screamed again. "No," I comforted. "Wake up and see me. It's Emily."

He whimpered now, his eyes still closed. I continued to talk in calm tones. A long shadow appeared on the wall in front of me. Maximillian quickly crouched down beside me.

"Peter. Peter." His voice was strained. "Let Papa hold you."

The child stopped thrashing, then started to mumble. "Don't make me . . . Don't want any . . ."

"What don't you want?" Maximillian asked soothingly. "Tell Papa."

"The smell . . . put the candle away."

"There isn't one here, *mein schatz*. Wake up. You're in your room."

But the lad was still dreaming. "Mustn't throw up. Mustn't." He shuddered violently, clapping his hand to his mouth. "No."

"Do you feel sick, Peter? Answer Papa."

The boy shook his head. His lips quivered. "Afraid."

"Of what?" Max turned to me. "What does he mean?"

"I don't know," I whispered.

Maximillian took his son in his arms. "There's nothing to fear. It's just a bad dream." He stroked Peter's cheek. "Come, now."

For some moments the boy's limbs remained tense, but they began to relax when Max gently rubbed them. "Papa, is it you? Really you?"

"See for yourself, *mein liebling.*"

Peter slowly opened his eyes. He gazed up at his father and blinked.

"Just me and Miss Hopkins who heard you."

The child glanced at me, then leaned against his father's arm. "It came back, Papa. It came again."

"But nothing happened. It's not real."

"It seems so real."

"Dreams can," his father said simply.

"Make it go away for good, Papa."

I watched as Max held his son and kissed the top of his head. I heard him sing softly, repeating the same phrase over and over. I saw Peter's hesitant smile become grateful. His eyelids grew heavy and dusted his cheeks. "There, now," Max whispered. "It's gone. All gone . . . forever."

Would it be? I knew how persistent nightmares were. I knew their power, and I felt sorry for the boy. He was sleeping again, thanks to his papa, and this made me think of my father . . . my closeness with him . . . my own demons. I rose to leave.

"Don't go yet, Miss Hopkins," Max entreated.

"He's all right now," I replied, my back to him.

"I want to thank you."

"It was nothing, truly."

"You got here before I did."

"My room is closer."

"Turn around so I can tell you something."

I did as bidden.

"You're very kind, you know."

I shied away from the compliment. "It's easy to help Peter. He's a wonderful boy."

Maximillian nodded wearily. "But a troubled one."

"I see that."

"If only he would tell me. If only he would open up and describe his dream, maybe we could do more than comfort him." His voice was tense. "Wait, you'll see how it is tomorrow morning. He won't want to talk about it."

"Maybe he can't. He may not remember."

"That's what he says, but the way he says it makes me think he's afraid to remember . . . afraid to speak up."

I could sympathize with this.

"I can't decipher his ramblings," the man went on, exasperated. "They make no sense. The boy doesn't sleep, and he doesn't eat. I'm worried sick."

"I am so sorry," I replied. "I'll do what I can to draw him out."

"Yes, you and he have a good understanding. I'm grateful . . . more than I can ever say."

He turned to his child and pulled the covers over him, caressing his cheek once more. When Max looked back to me, his face was dark with despair. It looked as if he would say something, but the line of his mouth stayed straight and firm. For another heart-stopping moment he returned my gaze, and only then did I notice that he wore an open shirt under his robe. Tied tight at his waist, it emphasized his wide shoulders, his proud carriage. I looked away, embarrassed by the direction of my thoughts.

Maximillian took a step closer, saying nothing. A silence fell between us, and when I collected myself enough to meet his gaze again, he was smiling rather sadly.

"Good night, Miss Hopkins," he said softly.

"Sleep well, Dr. Schaller."

I left in a daze. I wondered about the child and hoped I could help him. He sounded as if he didn't want to be pushed to do something he did not want to do. We all encouraged him to eat. Were we forcing him? Is that what brought the bad dreams on? He mentioned a candle and smell. How did they relate to his loss of appetite? It seemed he was afraid of vomiting. Why, if he was not sick? I wondered how long he had suffered from nightmares and where his mother was when they occurred. Where was she tonight? True, I was in her rooms. But she had never used them, Hannelore said. Would she have run if she heard her son's screams? I wasn't sure.

I was certain, though, that the child felt loved by his father. Poor man, so strong and yet so worried . . . and lonely.

✝ Chapter Six

I met with Dr. Demel much later than usual the following morning. He did not have to rummage through the pages on his desk for long before finding his notebook. But during the search, his gaze lingered upon an opened letter with an ink blot far in its lower left corner. It was a much-fingered piece of paper, and it was from a bank. I thought I saw some vague discomfort on his face before he slid the vellum sheet under several others. Drawing a breath, he smiled.

"Ready, Miss Hopkins?"

"Yes."

"Where were we?"

"My father's trip to Vienna."

"Quite, quite. But I know that period of his life," he said dismissively. "Let's take up before it, then proceed to the point just after. . . ." He cleared his throat. "I'm curious to know how he developed an interest in illnesses of the mind."

"I told you, my mother's death played a role in that."

"He suffered, poor man."

"More than most, I think, now that I examine that period so carefully."

"What do you mean?"

"I noticed that for the first time in his life he was reluctant to get out of bed on Sundays. I would have to coax him to get up."

"Was he moody?"

"Sometimes, yes. He appeared distracted. But by late afternoon and evening he seemed himself again."

"Was he often like this?"

"I don't know. I can't remember. But even Mrs. Reilly, our housekeeper, noticed it. She told me he was tired, overworked and needed the rest. She was a comfort to me."

"How long was he so distraught?"

"Months."

"Would you say he was melancholic?"

"Knowing what I do now . . . yes."

"Did he still have these bouts after his trip to Vienna?"

"On and off."

"How did they affect his practice?"

"Not much, I think. How could I really know? I was in school during the day. He never wanted for patients. I saw this in the summers when I visited their homes with him."

"He included you in his work, then?"

"Absolutely. We were close, and he encouraged my interest in the healing arts."

"And what of his dreams to have his own clinic?"

"We shared them. The plan was that after my apprenticeship with him I would go to medical school to learn the most recent scientific advances. After graduation and a residency we would run the clinic together."

"Was he a good preceptor?"

"The best."

"How so?"

"He was a keen observer, always studying the way a patient looked, always measuring his temperature and respiration. My father taught me to look for minute changes, to be cautious and deliberate. Above all, he taught me to listen."

"He inspired confidence in his patients." It was a statement, not a question.

"*That,* my father would say, "was part of the healing," I replied. "Emotions work through the mind and can influence the body."

"Would you say his own dips in mood were proof?"

"Definitely."

The clock on the desk struck noon just then, and I was grateful to leave the discussion here. Dr. Demel and I were rapidly approaching my most painful memories, my rawest wounds.

In the hall outside Dr. Demel's office, Peter's tutor swept by the butler, mumbling apologies to Maximillian, even to me, in his distracted state.

"It couldn't be helped. The axle broke," Herr Blitzer explained.

I took this to mean Peter had not yet had his morning lessons, and I had to work at masking a smile. The boy was probably thrilled at the reprieve from his schoolwork.

"My son is upstairs," Maximillian told him, smiling. "Go right up. He's waiting."

"With fingers and toes crossed," I added, half under my breath.

Maximillian came toward me, lips twitching. "The lad is hoping for a cancellation, no doubt of it," he whispered. Then to the tutor he said, "Don't stand on ceremony, Herr Blitzer. Run on up."

"Killjoy," I mouthed to Max behind the tutor's back.

His laugh was rich and hearty. "I'm off to buy Else Schleyer's birthday gift. Would you like to join me?"

I had not left the sanitarium grounds since my arrival. I could scarcely contain my pleasure at his invitation. "I would be delighted. Thank you."

"Can you meet me here in half an hour?"

"I'll be ready sooner," I assured him, and dashed up the stairs. Did my feet touch the steps?

I changed into a sapphire blue walking suit trimmed in black marten. My hat and parasol were the same deep blue, and my gloves were black. It took me longer than I anticipated to dress for the outing, but Maximillian didn't seem to mind the delay. When he saw me, in fact, his eyes sparkled with approval.

"You look marvelous," he whispered, helping me into the carriage. "Ooops, careful of the foot warmer," he cautioned, one strong arm steadying me.

"Do you think we'll need that?" I asked.

"I doubt it. It's lovely today."

Off we went, through the gates with the gilded *D* and down the hill toward the city's center.

"Are we going to the Ringstrasse?" I asked.

He smiled at me warmly. "If you wish."

"I haven't been there since I was twelve. I'd like to see it again, but only if it suits your shopping plans," I quickly added.

His chuckle was low and mellow. "It does."

Just then he removed his hat, set it on his lap, and smoothed back his hair with his fingers. He was an outrageously attractive man, and I couldn't help but admire the strength of his features, especially his arresting blue eyes. The expression in them was intense, yet subtly warm and teasing. He looked every bit the prominent physician, the gracious gentleman. His black frock coat outlined the breadth of his shoulders, and his stiff white collar and dark tie emphasized the healthy glow of his skin.

"I have one or two stores in mind for Else's gift," he said reassuringly, "and they're just off the Ringstrasse."

"That's a relief," I replied.

He taught me a great deal as we drove along, talking enthusiastically and amiably about the treasures in the village churches and the specialties of the wine gardens as we passed them. Many people had come out on this glorious day. Whether on foot or in carriages, their numbers grew, and an infectious liveliness seemed to fill the air about us.

Up ahead I could see the soaring spire of the cathedral. I saw tree-lined streets busy with trams and adorned with buildings that were enormous and magnificent. We paused at the next corner and watched a band march by, all gleaming sabers and high-stepping boots. We heard a bark of command, then music, heroic and stirring.

Here was the city as I remembered it—grand, varied, and charming. Tingling delight must have shown on my face, for when I turned to Maximillian I found him watching me, bemused. Coloring at my childish enthusiasm over a parade, of all things, I stammered, "It's silly of me . . . I didn't mean—"

"Don't," he whispered hoarsely. "Don't apologize." A slow, appreciative smile spread across his face, and I felt my heart make a sudden little bump.

Then we were on the fabled Ringstrasse, the boulevard that circled the city. I couldn't have uttered a sound if I wanted to now; the grandeur was breathtaking.

"The Ring," Max announced, "*the* symbol of Vienna's pride and Hapsburg permanency."

I didn't know where to look first. Majestic public buildings, ornate fountains, omnibuses. Chestnut and lime trees on either side of immense widths of cobblestone. Women selling flowers, public porters, barrel organs, elegantly dressed strollers promenading, watching, waiting to see and be seen. An astounding display of pomp and wealth!

"This must rival Paris," I whispered.

"The Emperor's intention, no doubt."

Our carriage stopped, and Maximillian went on. "In 1857 the Emperor decided to have this street built. It's shaped like a horseshoe with both ends meeting the Danube canal."

I pointed to my right. "These look like official buildings."

"They are. I'll explain a bit first and then we'll have a look around." With new delight he gestured with one hand and used the other to gently turn my shoulders so I faced the proper direction. "The Parliament, City Hall, court of law, and parts of the Imperial Palace are used for politics, while the museums, the University, the Opera, theaters, and concert hall are dedicated to the arts."

"The Viennese take culture seriously. It's wonderful."

"You'll hear music everywhere. It's as important and plentiful as air to all Viennese, rich or poor. Whether they're in the park, beer garden, or at the Philharmonic, the public expects a superior performance. Same holds true in the theater," he continued in the same proud tone. "The first pages people turn to when they pick up their morning papers are reviews and featured articles of actors and actresses. They're the pampered darlings of society. If one of them dies, the whole city mourns—even those who can't read," he added with a smile.

"You must love living here. Your life is so enriched."

"It could be better, Miss Hopkins." There was a sudden, undeniable tone of regret in his voice.

I knew what he meant. He shared little with his wife. I didn't want to look at him. I saw that lonely, vulnerable expression I had seen last night in Peter's room. He was a married man, I told myself. I must not show my sympathy, must not encourage him. But this was getting harder to do.

"Did you grow up here?" I asked, trying to get the conversation on a more neutral plane.

"Pretty much." He sighed. "My father was a physician. Someday I'll show you where his office was, but now back to my tour." He wiggled his eyebrows. "Am I doing a good job?"

"I'm fascinated, Dr. Schaller. Best tour I've had since I came."

His reply was a low, rumbling laugh. "You mean the *only* one you've had since you came."

A passerby paused and waved, and Maximillian tipped his hat.

"These buildings are incredibly impressive," I said. "The architecture, heavy and ornate . . ."

"You noticed," he answered, his tone becoming ironic. "And you might have a hard time identifying the styles. They practically run the gamut from antiquity to the present day."

"What do you mean?"

He gestured broadly. "The Parliament building looks like a Greek temple. The Opera House was patterned after a Renaissance palace. The University resembles a French castle, and in City Hall there are influences of English Gothic. There's no grand design. It's a confusion of tastes. One incredible mishmash, if you ask me."

"How did it happen?"

"The architects of the Ringstrasse purposely imitated other styles, but they exaggerated and corrupted them. Everything had to be opulent, overdone. Everything had to be for show," he said sarcastically.

"I don't understand."

"Wait until you see the apartment buildings of the wealthy on this street. Then you will. Those homes have more curlicues than a wedding cake." His voice rose. "The whole Ringstrasse is a monument to the indulgence of the people who built here—the nouveau riche bourgeois who ape the lifestyle of the aristocrats."

I was surprised at the condescension in his tone. "You're upset," I commented.

"How can I not be? I'm bitter, too. I'm talking about my in-laws, Miss Hopkins. Wait until you see their house. It's got more stone garlands and sculptured gewgaws per square centimeter than a horse has hairs." With a dark scowl, Maximillian shouted to the driver to move the carriage forward.

I saw what he meant by excess. It was flaunted here by the wealthy. But they did nurture the arts. Surely, this was to their credit. I said as much.

"Of course they foster culture," Max replied. "They exalt in it and even see themselves as the cultural torchbearers to the next generation. But their actions are more for their own glorification than anything else," he said grimly.

We had left behind the public buildings and were approaching patrician homes, one larger and more lavish than the next.

"This Ringstrasse is a showpiece of capitalism," my companion went on. "It's a symbol of the new wealth and newly won privileges of the German-speaking bourgeoisie. They won the right to vote and can run their own courts, but they refuse to allow the lower classes and other nationalities to do the same." He shook his head gravely. "The poor have it hard here. More and more evictions take place every month, and people drag carts full of their worldly possessions through the city while they search for other places to live."

So that was what I had witnessed the night of my arrival. I was fascinated by Max's account of Vienna and touched by his concern for the displaced.

"The sorry truth is," he continued, "that while the newly rich industrialists celebrate their rewards to the fullest, they deceive themselves. I fear, Miss Hopkins, that time might prove the Viennese fable to be flawed."

We drove on in silence for a while.

As any visitor would, I observed the grandeur, elegance, and all the finery. But Max's revelations made me think differently about the glamorous people getting in and out of the endless line of highly lacquered coaches.

Iris' people, according to Max.

I looked at his face. His expression was still, taut. Such an intense, idealistic man. A man who held his beliefs passionately. How different he was from his frivolous wife. I wondered how she had convinced him to build her a house here on the Ringstrasse if he viewed these things with such contempt.

Maybe he had to. A divorce would be difficult to obtain. Maybe living apart at times was the only way they both could be sane. She was to move here with Friedericke to keep up appearances, I supposed. This way her husband would come home occasionally to visit her son. She and her husband would go out together socially. Only their close friends would know. It would be a life of pretense. A sham.

It would kill Maximillian.

Aware of my scrutiny, he turned to me. "What are you thinking?"

I hesitated.

"I'm curious. Tell me."

"Well, I was wondering where the new apartment is. Iris' house."

"It's on the other side. I try to avoid it. But you can get some idea of what it's like if you look at the facade of the building we're just now passing. Notice how it is heavily festooned? See the leaves above the doors? That's a motif from Greek gravestones which my wife insisted her stonemasons copy," he added wryly.

It was a grandiose home, a palace with an overdecorated exterior. It also looked outrageously expensive. How could the

Demel clinic provide enough money to support this construction? How could Max? He said his in-laws were rich. Was the Demel family independently wealthy—the doctor, Friedericke, and Werner?

As if reading my thoughts, Maximillian continued. "These homes typify the values of the rising commercial class. Take Iris' father. He started out owning a piano factory. As his profits increased, he invested capital into other ventures: railroads, real estate, tobacco, farm equipment. He became exceedingly wealthy, to the boundless delight of his wife. There was suddenly enough money to climb the social ladder. And up they went!"

My companion was getting excited again. I wondered about the wisdom and the etiquette of prompting him to speak of his relatives, but he seemed determined to get something off his chest.

"I rue the day I met them . . . and their daughter."

"How did you?" I blurted out.

"Riding. Iris is an accomplished equestrienne." He went on briskly. "Let me tell you one story. I hope it will put matters into perspective."

I touched his sleeve. "I don't mean to pry . . . really."

"But you're curious about her, aren't you?"

I nodded.

"And about . . . me?" I thought I heard his voice quaver. "I would like to think that . . . Emily." His eyes were imploring, his voice husky. "May I call you Emily?"

"Yes," I answered softly.

Gazing at me, he drew a long breath and then began. "Iris' parents fostered the worst qualities in her. They raised her to feel superior to others. They told her she was named after Iris, the goddess of rainbows. They instilled in her a false sense of importance by telling her that rainbows span the air between earth and sky, that they represent the relationship between the gods and man." Max's voice was harsh. "Can you imagine raising a child with these notions?"

This explained the long blue glass in his wife's room. I

remembered being struck the moment I saw this work of art. It was an exquisite portrayal of the Greek goddess gliding down her rainbow.

"Her parents were not *too* grandiose," Max added, his tone sarcastic. "Ironically, the goddess is often depicted holding the caduceus—the symbol of the medical profession. But Iris refused to let the artist, who created the piece you see in her room, put the caduceus in the goddess' hand." His voice sank to a caustic whisper. "My wife has nothing but contempt for those who need healing. They're misfits, according to her." He inhaled sharply. "So it started with her name, this narcissism, and it grew as she grew, carefully nurtured by her mother and father. They worked at building her image socially. Made sure she moved in the right circles. Had the right education. They even saw to it that their darling's achievements frequently made the newspapers." Sighing heavily, Maximillian finished, "I met her shortly after the head of the famous Spanish Riding School was quoted in the society pages, praising her horsemanship."

"But didn't you see her self-centeredness?" Perhaps it was more than I should have said, but Max didn't seem to mind.

"Iris masks it well when she wants to," he answered. "She can be deceitful. She puts on a childlike voice. She purposely tries to let people think she likes them, but when their backs are turned, she'll say dreadfully unkind things about them."

"As she did with Frau Schleyer?"

"Yes. That's why I'm buying the woman a gift."

From the Ringstrasse we turned into Karntnerstrasse, a street lined with exclusive shops. The carriage came to a stop at an elegant entrance. Inside we were welcomed by the owner. He graciously showed us porcelain animals, richly engraved smelling bottles, and sterling whistles. Saying no to each, Max walked toward an antique writing desk, picked up the tall floor vase next to it, and turned to me. "What do you think?"

"Does she like oriental things?"

"I once heard her compliment Iris about something similar at our house. Anyway, I'm partial to blue." At that moment his gaze went to my walking suit and then lingered upon my face, touching each feature with care.

"May I interest you in this dragon vase?" The proprietor's voice came from behind me, yet it seemed distant.

"Wrap both," Maximillian replied absently.

As soon as the salesman went to the rear of his store, Max whispered, "I fear we're causing a scene."

I felt my cheeks stain with color and could only answer, "I hope not."

Someone else came into the shop, a plump elderly lady. The fuchsia feathers on her hat hid much of her face. *Friedericke?* Maximillian's eyebrows went up, his lips curved into a smile. For a panic-stricken moment I wondered if she had witnessed the exchange between her nephew and me. She turned slowly to greet the proprietor.

"Frau Wentz!" he exclaimed.

I sagged with relief.

Max took his packages. We were back in the carriage. I still felt embarrassed and began to worry. *That's the way of it. That's what it's like with a married man. That's what I can always expect.*

It was as if a cloud had settled over us. The excitement of the afternoon was gone. Max sensed my mood and tried to lighten it.

"My preference for blue stops with that," he said, pointing to a poodle strutting on the sidewalk with his master.

Except for a tuft of gray at the end of its tail, another topping each ear, and four "socks" of the color on its legs, the animal appeared blue, dark blue.

"So closely shaven," I said in amazement.

"Within an inch of his life." Max chuckled.

"Is that the style here, to let the veins show?" I was still staring at the dog.

"Who knows?" Max shrugged. "Next month some other idea will catch on."

The ride home seemed much too short. Our outing was coming to an end, our time together slipping away. Max seemed tired and tense. We spoke little. Once, when the carriage took a sharp turn, Maximillian leaned against me. "Sorry," he said, but he never moved away after the conveyance stabilized itself.

I was secretly glad. I liked the feel of his strong arm next to mine. I rested my head on the back of the cushioned seat. My eyelids grew heavy. If I let my eyes close, if I pretended to sleep, I could still touch him. I wouldn't be obliged to keep a polite space between us. I shut my eyes.

Bliss.

There was regret in Maximillian's voice when next I heard it. "We're almost there."

The view from the carriage window proved him right. Up ahead were the heavy gates with the gilded *D*. For Demel or . . . devil?

From its lofty heights, the sanitarium looked down on us gloomily. I remembered the coachman's warning, the box-wood bushes in the topiary garden, the mechanical piece I had found buried in a box stored in the passageway. I thought of the strained atmosphere in the palace. The peculiar Dr. Demel. The sly Werner. The troubled child, Peter. The threatening atmosphere. Hard as I tried, I could not shake the dread I felt in returning.

"I wish we weren't here." It was my own half whisper.

"I know," came the bleak reply.

My dark thoughts about the household were again justified soon after our arrival. Slouched against a wall in the entry hall fingering his mustache, Werner's eyes brightened when he saw me. He brought forward a newspaper that was half hidden behind him.

"Have you seen this?" he asked coolly.

My inclination was to ignore him, but he stepped into the middle of the hall, blocking my way. His smile was secretive. "Don't you read the advertisements?"

An innocuous subject I thought. I'd humor him and leave. "No, not unless I'm looking to buy something."

"Much is offered . . . and sought, Miss Hopkins. Dare I

entertain you?" His tone was faintly mocking.

I didn't reply.

"The classified ads can be personal and quite illuminating." His eyes scanned the print. "I quote:

"The gentleman who tripped most clumsily on his dog's leash on the Kärntnerstrasse yesterday and who heard such endearing kindness in the voice of the enchantress wearing the stunning red outfit . . . said gentleman begs to erase any lingering concerns this lady's goodness may cause her at a meeting he prays will take place at her earliest convenience. Reply Box 503, this newspaper."

"What?"

Werner read on.

"To the fascinating lady holding her white cat while exiting Schneider's flower shop yesterday: Is she aware that upon her departure from said shop the lovely blooms inside, despairing of their competition, wilted miserably? If such lady would grant this appreciative gentleman a chance to gaze upon the fairest blossom of all, he promises her a veritable garden of delights. Please reply, Box 742, this newspaper."

Werner looked up. "Expressed with typical Viennese panache, wouldn't you agree, Miss Hopkins?"

"Of what interest are such silly flirtations to me?"

"Oh, but they should be," he said. "People read these nuggets of information every day. Then they discuss them."

"Who has time for such nonsense?"

"Iris, for one."

"Does she search for herself in these columns?" I shot back.

Werner carefully folded the paper and placed it under his arm. Thrusting his hands in his pockets, he leaned against the wall. "My, my," he said coolly, "the little dove has teeth."

"I'll be on my way, Herr Demel," I replied, stepping past him.

Another snicker. "Around here, Miss Hopkins, some people send fictitious descriptions to the newspaper, just to fuel gossip. A word to the wise: Never put yourself in a vulnerable position vis à vis the tongue waggers."

"What does it matter, then, if people know falsehoods are spread in this way?" Not waiting for a reply, I hastened on, hearing his churlish laugh until I turned the corner at the corridor's far end.

Though I disliked Werner, this recent encounter set me to wondering. I had spent the afternoon in the city with Maximillian Schaller. Alone with him—for all to see. Werner, no doubt, learned of it and, out of jealousy, tried to alarm me. I must not do it again. It wasn't smart, and it wasn't right. I was critical of Iris for being an adulteress. If I coveted her husband, was I any better?

With this sobering thought I resolved to behave more circumspectly with Max. I would go out with him no more and would put an end to our private exchanges. From now on I would be polite and discreet with the handsome doctor. I had, after all, a commitment here in Vienna that I could not—would not—jeopardize.

Later that evening something happened that made me more resolute, but also more frightened.

It was not quite dark. I was on my bed, going through my father's journals, reviewing his descriptions of the way asylums were organized in America. Not seeing my lamp, and assuming it had been removed, I crossed the hall in search of another. I entered a small drawing room, pleasant in the fading light of day, and curled up with the diary on a chair by the window.

The gardens at the entrance below were strangely still. The dry leaves of autumn lay motionless on the graveled drive where the slightest breeze would normally ruffle and swirl them. No horse, or coach, or footman waited. No bird flashed from bough to bough. My gaze circled the silent scene. And then to the right I saw a shadow, a tall, lengthening shadow, spilling across a bench. Curious now, my fingers grasped more

of the lacy curtain, expanding my view. There stood a man.
  Maximillian.
He strode toward the bench, restless and tense. He ruthlessly
kicked at the grass. Something hung limply from his tightened
fist—a scrap of material, something dark. I watched as he
brought it close to his face. I watched him study . . . my glove.
With tender fingers he opened its cuff, his expression taut and
despairing. Unable to breathe, I watched him close his eyes,
lower his cheek to the soft leather and gently caress it.
  In that moment of joyous awareness, I could not move.
Dared not move. I must not be seen. Dazed and flushed, I
stared across to a window on the floor below.
  There was a movement so slight that I would have missed
it, had my gaze not been so fixed. My eyes narrowed. Did the
curtain there sway?
  I hurriedly released the lace from my own hand and sat
stiffly in the chair. A frisson of fear worked its way through
my bones.
  As twilight deepened, I remained in that chair. Soon the
outside lamps were lit, casting shadows in the drawing room.
They danced and taunted, teased and mocked until my thoughts
spun in confusion. Yet I sat there without a light, listening to
the sounds of the house.
  Each was sad.
  And filled with warning.

✝ Chapter Seven

I was grateful when Dr. Demel suggested a tour of the sanitarium the next day. I would have welcomed any opportunity to postpone the discussion of the most painful chapter of my father's life and mine, and I wanted to visit the clinic. My host's offer served both purposes. I quickly accepted.

"You'll find it different from an American hospital, Miss Hopkins, but I'm hoping you can assist us. Tell us how your father would have organized his private clinic, had he been able to establish one."

"My pleasure, Dr. Demel."

It had been many weeks since I'd been in a hospital, and I could feel a stir of excitement as we approached it. "How many patients do you have?" I asked.

"The census is low right now. Twenty or so."

"How do you select them?"

"We don't have anyone here who is violent or a threat to his community. The patients are troublesome to their families, disruptive, that's all."

"You mean they embarrass them."

"Sometimes."

"Can they wash and dress and feed themselves?"

"Most do, yes."

"What kinds of symptoms do they have?"

"Some are gloomy, not wanting to exert themselves in any

way. Others are easily upset, set off by the slightest thing. Heart palpitations. Fears of suffocation." He smiled. "The specifics vary. We have more than neurasthenia cases here now."

He waited for me to ask another question, but when I saw the word *Klinik* above a wide, metal door, I realized we had taken a different route to the clinic than I had the night I overheard Iris and her lover. "Is there another entrance?" I asked.

"Yes, near the family wing. Dr. Schaller and I use it," he answered, jangling his keys.

"Is the other door locked, too?"

"Yes, but the family has keys because the entrance is near Friedericke's solarium." He held the door while I stepped inside. "Her flowers have a healing influence on the patients. On the days they work with plants, they're like new people. It's wonderful."

I was surprised to note that the reception area was not large or open, and the lanky, tight-lipped matron on duty was not as friendly as I would have liked.

"Anything new, Bertha?" the hospital director inquired.

She nodded. "It's Frau Steinmetz, Dr. Demel. She's having a bad day. And two of the attendants are arguing over which patients they're responsible for. Neither one wants Herr Baumer. He's too difficult. Causes fights, they say."

"I'll start with that problem, Bertha. Where's the staff?"

"In the office, talking, I hope."

"Would you show Miss Hopkins around, meantime?"

Bertha grimaced but led me down the hall.

I didn't see more than three or four patients. "Where is everyone?" I asked.

"What do you mean?"

I remembered Peter once saying that his father encouraged inmates to go outdoors and get some exercise. "The other patients." I asked, "Are they outside?"

"A few are."

The numbers weren't adding up—at least not to the twenty Dr. Demel mentioned. As the director of the institution, wouldn't he know the exact number of patients and their names at any given time? They didn't come to the clinic for an overnight visit. In most instances they stayed for months.

The walls were white, nondescript, but clean. The few pictures on them were small and grouped together. All of them were green, giving the impression of a flowing meadow or spreading ferns. My gaze didn't stay on them long. I felt drawn to the frail woman sitting by herself beneath the pictures.

"It's Frau Steinmetz," Bertha whispered to me. She was about to add something, but I shook my head to discourage her. I didn't like discussing patients in their presence. It was demeaning.

Bertha studied me with glittering eyes. I wondered for a moment if she was now biting back some opinion of me.

I smiled ever so slightly.

The matron's eyebrows lifted, and with an awkward pivot she stiffly walked off.

"Frau Steinmetz," I said quietly.

The woman stared ahead, gloomy and silent.

I sat beside her.

"Frau Steinmetz," I began again, this time looking at the embroidery in her delicate hands. "That's a lovely flower. Is it edelweiss?"

She shook her head. Barely.

"I don't mean to intrude," I told her, "but I'm very fond of wildflowers, and I couldn't help but notice—"

"Where's Dr. Schaller?" she muttered.

I couldn't answer exactly. I didn't know where Maximillian was. "He'll return," I said, "but I'm not sure when."

"It's never the same without him," she mumbled dejectedly, pushing aside her needlework.

"You miss him," I said sympathetically.

Pale gray eyes turned up to me, the prettiest feature in her gaunt face. "The Lord's own, he is."

The poor woman looked weary, worn to the bone. Her hair

was pulled back, accentuating her thinness. Her cheeks were pale. Pain and suffering were etched on her face.

"Whom are you visiting?" she asked.

"No one. I'm here to tour the hospital," I replied. "I have no family here."

"Are you a doctor?" She sounded surprised by my explanation.

"Not yet."

"It was all too much for me," she whined.

"I'm sorry."

"I couldn't do it, and now God is punishing me."

"For what?" I asked quietly.

"Not being a good daughter. Not doing my work at the church."

"You sound so sad."

She nodded. "Sick inside . . . in my heart and soul. That's where the devil is now."

"Why do you think you were not a good daughter?"

"My father is old and bedridden. He has no one else. I was up all night. I got tired," she said despairingly. "Couldn't do it anymore."

"And now you think you must not be a good person."

"Yes. This torment of my soul is punishment."

"Is that what Dr. Schaller says?"

"No."

"What does he tell you?"

"That I was overworked . . . and . . ."

"Go on."

"And that if I believe the soul lives forever, it can't be diseased and die like the body." A hint of a smile softened the lines in her face. "He tells me that God has not abandoned me and that I should eat and rest and get strong again."

When I smiled at the woman and held her hand, slim fingers gripped mine. "You're kind," she murmured. "Thank you."

"Well, Frau Steinmetz." It was Dr. Demel's voice. "Still knitting, I see."

Did her frail back stiffen in Demel's presence?

"Embroidering, Professor Doctor," she corrected, holding up her work.

"Yes, of course," he answered, embarrassed.

He took my arm and guided me toward another room, a smaller one. When we were inside, he closed the door. "She suffers terribly from melancholia. What did you say to make her smile?"

"It's more what Dr. Schaller said, not me. Where is he today?"

"He went to hear Dr. Freud lecture. I wish he were here. I could use his help."

"Whose? Dr. Freud's or Dr. Schaller's?"

My host laughed. "Both."

"But there aren't enough patients to cause that much trouble."

"Sometimes it takes just one or two. The fellow down the hall is extremely negative. He opposes everything any of us say to him."

"For instance?"

"When I greeted him by his name, 'How are you, Herr Baumer?' he replied, 'I am not a man. My name is Frau Muller.' And when I casually mentioned that it was a nice day, he told me flat out it was not."

"Did you suggest he go outside and see the sunshine?"

"Yes. Guess what he answered."

"That it was raining."

"Right."

"Is he anxious?" I asked.

"Very," Dr. Demel said with a nod. "And rigid. A most difficult case. But please let me take you through the rest of the ward."

At the far end of the floor we entered the solarium. Panels of glass surrounded us. Sunlight streamed through, drenching potted trees and tiers of tropical flowers with warmth. The sound of water trickled in a fountain, and the smell of fresh earth and blossoms filled the air.

A tall young man, oblivious to our presence, stopped to pick up a small pile of weeds. He smiled at Friedericke who had her back to us. Standing regally by the fountain, waving a calla lily, she might well have been sprinkling stardust, so lovely and tranquil did the tableau appear.

Dr. Demel beamed at the sight. "The smartest thing we ever did was to build a new conservatory for Friedericke here."

"Where was the old one?" I asked quietly.

"Attached to the back of the family wing."

Friedericke turned sharply, setting a wayward curl bobbing. "Franz!" she exclaimed. "It's you . . . and Miss Hopkins." The lily stem swished through the air in a dramatic flourish. "Come in, come in."

Her brother laughed. "We can return when you're not so busy."

"Nonsense," she replied, tucking a hand beneath my arm. Pointing with the drooping white flower, she went on. "These are my prize orchids. Those, my gardenias. And that tree over there is breathtaking in bloom. It's a crabapple," she said, sighing.

Enchanted, I let my gaze wander about this crystal room. Over the nasturtium, past the tall sea grass, down to the violets and small bedding plants. There was a low hedge, a border, and then some unusual-looking blossoms. "Is that hibiscus?"

"Oh, no," she said. "They and the camellias are by the entrance. Did you miss them?" She turned to the young man who was chatting with Dr. Demel. "They're Johann's favorites."

At the mention of his name, Johann looked up. Once again I was surprised. The man before me had fine features, expressive hazel eyes, a sensitive face.

Iris' lover?

His smile faded under my study, and I, embarrassed, tried to make amends. "The flowers are lovely," I said.

Friedericke looked as proud as a mother hen. "He's my best gardener," she said, her dimples deepening. "I'm grateful. My garden has never looked better."

And neither has she, I realized. There was more than pleasure in her expression. More than satisfaction. There was a kind of radiance, especially in her eyes. I had never seen them so bright.

She squeezed my hand, appearing to look behind me. "Uh-oh, here's trouble."

All eyes went to Bertha.

For several moments the matron stood there, holding her bottom lip between her teeth as if she were hesitant to speak.

"Is something wrong?" asked Dr. Demel.

"It's Herr Kirsch. He's not feeling well."

"I'll be there in a minute," said Demel.

I went with the director to Herr Kirsch's room. His elderly face had drained of color, and beads of perspiration formed on his upper lip. He complained of thirst and a headache, of feeling sick, yet he was excitedly pacing the floor, despite his advanced years.

"So, where's my schnapps?" he barked. "What do I have to do to get one? Julia and I always have schnapps."

He spoke so fast I could hardly understand him.

"What did he say?" I asked Dr. Demel.

"Well, now, would you look at this," Herr Kirsch went on, staring at me. "A feast for the eyes next to big-footed Bertha. My, yes, this one's a looker. I can pick them. Always could. Had a few in my day." He barely paused for breath. "I'm going to take over this place and run it right for you, Dr. Demel, and first thing I do is get rid of the old battle-ax and set up a beer garden near the greenhouse." His finger jabbed the air for emphasis. "Awful hot here. I'm burning up. Open the windows!"

Studying the poor, agitated man, I noticed his pupils were widely dilated. "What can we do for him?" I whispered to Demel.

"Give him an opiate to calm him down. The elderly often become confused."

So saying, the director found Bertha, wrote down his orders, and announced to me that it was time to leave.

We exited through the family entrance, as Demel called it, and my host became chattier than ever.

"I plan to expand, Miss Hopkins. We have room for at least fifty patients. I believe in the humane treatment of the mentally ill, pioneered by Pinel in France and Tuke in England, but I want to learn more about the way American doctors organize their asylums. They're more advanced in this regard."

"Thanks to the tireless efforts of Dorthea Dix and the new frontiers established by Dr. Kirkbride in Philadelphia," I said. "That man's work will influence the whole profession."

"I was intrigued by his ideas when your father described them. Did you ever visit Kirkbride's hospital?"

"Yes, with my father. And after his death I worked there as a companion to several patients before I came here."

"Tell me your impressions of the Kirkbride asylum."

"It's a haven for people who are dreadfully afflicted with mental illness."

"So I understand."

"The patients are encouraged to get their minds off themselves, to be active and cheerful. The entire staff promotes this attitude. So do the surroundings. The architecture of the building, the inside layout, the gardens, *calisthenium* for exercise, the music and reading rooms—all are designed to promote healing."

"I understand Dr. Kirkbride planned the overall program down to the last detail himself."

"Yes. He has absolute authority over all aspects of patient care. The entire staff, from his assistant physicians to the cook, answer to him."

"I like that. Tell me more."

"The patients who are well enough are taken into the city.

They learn about the newest inventions and hear lectures. The idea is to make them feel they are still connected to the outside world."

"This is truly progressive. But tell me, how are the most disturbed patients protected from themselves and from one another?"

"Physical restraints are used, but judiciously. So is morphine. It's not all a glowing picture, however. A number of patients have escaped and some have committed suicide. That provokes criticism from the community—even the medical community."

Dr. Demel grew thoughtful. "I can imagine. How is the hospital administered?"

We had entered the family wing now, so I quickly summarized the roles of the assistant physicians, the steward, matrons, and how they differed from the positions of the attendants and supervisors. Demel was fascinated.

"And you were a teacher there, you say?"

"Yes, a companion. I organized group activities, read aloud to the patients, planned social events, etcetera."

"Will you read to *me,* Miss Hopkins?" Peter's tentative voice quavered above the stack of books he carried. Standing by my chamber door, books piled to his chin, he was obviously waiting for me.

"Gladly, my friend," I replied.

Dr. Demel ruffled the boy's hair. Turning to me, he said, "It has been more than an interesting morning. I can't thank you enough, Miss Hopkins." There was a low, appreciative glimmer in his dark eyes. "You may well be . . . my salvation."

"Let's go in there," Peter suggested, leading the way into the small parlor and to the chair by the window—the one with the view out front. "My tutor says I should listen to other people read and then practice all by myself."

Lifting the books from his arms, I asked, "Where shall we start?"

"The top one."

"What's it about?"

"A dog."

"I like dogs. What's his name?"

"Hero, and he really is one."

"So, you know the story already."

"I read it a lot lately."

When we were settled in the chair, all snuggled up and cozy, I asked, "How's that?"

I felt his shoulders rise and fall, his nose nuzzle my arm. "I dunno."

"Tell me about Hero."

"He's not real."

"Most characters in books are imaginary."

"No, I mean even in the story he's not alive."

This was getting more interesting. "What is he?" I whispered.

"Stuffed."

I laughed. "Like a trout on the wall?"

"Miss Hopkins," he said reprovingly, lifting his soft cheek from my shoulder. "Don't you know there are toy animals? Haven't you seen them on my bed?"

"Oh, that kind," I replied, my tone warm and teasing. "Now, what did this cuddly creature do to deserve his name?"

"None of the other toys liked him. He sat all by himself on Dietrich's bed, sad and lonely. Dietrich never scolded his toy soldiers and their friends. Instead, he did more things with Hero. Took him everywhere. But most important, he held the dog when his mother read to him. And over time, Hero began to make sense of the letters. Put them together with sounds. He learned to read, Miss Hopkins."

"Smart dog."

"Just like me."

I took his chin in my hand and looked into deep blue eyes so full of hope and trust. "Yes," I agreed, "just like you." Then I bent my head and kissed him.

One small tear rolled down Peter's cheek. "You're nice," he whispered. "I'm glad you came."

"Me, too," I said, returning his hug.

Smiling, he went on. "Anyway, Hero saw a letter from Dietrich's teacher at school. There was going to be a collection of old toys for the poor, and all the children were asked to go through their toy chests and sort out what they wanted to keep and what they didn't."

"And because Hero could read, he knew something his fellow toys didn't," I said.

"That's right. Now he had to decide whether to tell the others to hide or not."

"The so-called friends that were never good to him."

Peter nodded.

"It must have been a difficult decision."

"It was."

"That's what happens when you have knowledge, Peter."

"What do you mean?"

"Knowledge brings responsibility. Poor Hero had to ask himself what was expected of him now that he had this information. He had to ask what he expected of himself. Was he going to do the right thing?"

"But what's right, Miss Hopkins? Sometimes it's hard to know." The boy seemed sad and puzzled. His face clouded as if he were thinking of something that he couldn't quite understand.

"What did Hero do?" I asked.

"He told his friends about the letter."

"He took the high road, then."

"What's that?"

"Never mind. Were they grateful?"

"Yes," Peter answered with a smile. "They called him Hero."

I laughed and tousled his hair. "Of course. But do you know what? We didn't read the story."

He was laughing with me when Iris appeared in the doorway. Then he said, "*I'll* read the next one, Miss Hopkins."

His mother stormed in. "You'll do nothing of the sort, young man. Get out of that chair this instant. We have things to do."

Peter didn't move.

"Did you hear me?" she said, louder.

"What things?" Peter asked, puzzled.

"When I tell you to do something," she snapped, reaching for him arm, "you had better do it."

"But I don't want to," the boy shouted, inching closer to me.

With one swift yank, she brought the boy to his feet. I saw him cringe as he watched his mother's hand arc back and sweep down toward him.

"Don't you dare!" Maximillian roared, as he came upon the scene, staying her arm.

"He's an impudent child," she spat, struggling in her husband's firm grasp.

"And I suppose you are the very breath of maternal kindness," he replied sarcastically, holding her still. His voice grew deathly quiet. "If you ever strike this child, you'll have me to answer to."

Peter began to sob.

Maximillian released his wife and pushed her aside. "Come here, son."

The lad flew into his father's arms.

This was no place for me, I realized. I got up to leave, wishing I had never allowed the boy to entice me to read with him. But he was a sad and lonely child, a beautiful one. *And* he needed me. It was this thought that allowed me to return Iris' hateful smile as I crossed the room.

From behind my chamber door I heard Max soothe his son.

"Miss Hopkins and I were reading. That's all, Papa," the child explained.

A few minutes later, he began to giggle, and when his laughter grew louder, I realized he was in the hall, just outside my door. I stepped back, thinking he would open it. But what he did instead was neatly pile his books there and leave.

"Really, Max." I heard Iris say. "Didn't you overdo it? Playing the great rescuer in front of the lovely Miss Hopkins?"

"The child only wanted someone to read to him . . . and

not finding his mother . . ." Maximillian let these last words hit home.

"Or his father," Iris pointed out coolly.

"Give it up, woman."

"How can you stoop so low to protect someone below your social station?"

"As I recall, dear wife, I was protecting my son."

"She'll bring you down, Max. I'm warning you."

I could scarcely credit my ears. Iris was admitting to her husband she was aware of his appreciation for me. But this didn't seem to bother her as much as the loss of social status I might cause him. I stepped closer to the door.

"How could it matter to you?" Max asked.

"You've never understood," she said. "As long as we're married, everything you do reflects on me."

Max laughed once harshly.

"Don't mock me," she said, imperiously. "Come opening night at the Burgtheater, I'm entering with the nobility. I've befriended a Russian count just for the purpose. That's the difference between us," she said. "I know where I'm going. *I* know who I am."

Max let those words fill the air.

"Show up at that entrance, madam, and you'll quickly find out who you are *not*," he spat.

For the rest of the afternoon my thoughts swirled through my mind like currents in a flood tide. Iris would not have reacted so violently to my reading with Peter if she were pleased with herself as a mother. She obviously felt guilty about the lack of time she spared for her son. But what about her role as wife? Perhaps I was reading too much into what she said, but she implied she would not be surprised if her husband enjoyed the attention of other females. It appeared she almost expected it, especially if the women were Max's social equals. If Iris cared one bit about her marriage, she didn't show it. Neither did Max. The life had gone out of their union. It was as dark and as dead as a candle wick in the rain.

This thought both haunted and heartened me. It churned through my mind during dinner, sang in my heart while I undressed for bed, drifted blissfully into my dreams. . . .

A man ran toward me, and I hastened to meet him. He caught me up and spun me around like some great wind. My hands gripped his shoulders firmly while he carried me out of the dim passage into the soft glow of a rose-hued room. He sat on a settee, taking me down with him, pressing me to him.

My slipper fell to the floor, a muffled bump from some far-off place. My eyelids fluttered down. My head fell back. My fingers splayed across his flesh. A whimper escaped my parted lips.

"Emily, look at me."

"No, no, it must not be."

Slowly he lifted my face toward his.

"Look at me," he implored.

I shook my head and heard him sigh deeply.

Tentatively his fingers stroked my cheek, feathered my temples, and brushed my lips and chin. His touch was incredibly soft, so heated and gentle, so masterfully light. I scarcely knew the exact moment he found the ribbons of my dressing gown, edging back its lace with care. He murmured soothingly then.

Shame rippled through me as he brought me to some new feeling, something until now unknown and indefinable, but powerful and lovely, nearly too lovely. His fingers greeted each new expanse of skin with reverence.

"Ohhh." I shivered. "I like that."

"I knew you would," he whispered back.

An exquisite tension began to build inside me, suffusing me with flaming heat. My half-closed eyes watched Max's head bend slowly and irrevocably toward me. With a tortured breath his lips parted. And then they found me.

All at once the whole room tilted.

Dawn's rosy fingers stole quietly under the window shutters, waking me gently. I closed my eyes, wanting to savor the glow of my reverie.

Yes, a dream!

But the dream, beautifully tender and haunting, was at once sweet and full of regret.

✝ Chapter Eight

After breakfast I returned to my chamber. The unmade bed surprised me because Hannelore usually tidied up by now. A strong fragrance filled my nostrils, causing me to glance at the dressing table. Had I forgotten to cap my perfume bottle? Then I saw the tiny velvet box containing the Civil War memento on the floor. How had it gotten there?

When I stooped to pick it up, I saw an envelope. Smooth clean vellum, so crisp-looking I thought it unused. But it was thick. With uncertain fingers I reached inside and removed a note.

Again, the minuscule lettering.

> Can you hear the devil's trumpet? Listen and be warned.

I stared at the message scrawled unevenly on the paper. I turned it over, looking for some identifying mark, some clue of its author.

Nothing, just the evil scrawl.

Who did this? Who entered my room? Who had a key? *Iris!* Of course, she was furious with me yesterday for reading to her son. She heard her husband protect me. How she must hate me. But I wondered if she would choose this quiet way of warning me. Given her nature, wouldn't she be bolder and more theatrical with her threats?

Perhaps Werner was the culprit. He knew I had been out with Max two days ago. He had read me the scandal sheets.

He was jealous, and I didn't think a poisoned pen would be beneath him.

But anyone could have seen us leave for the city and return hours later. Anyone could have observed Max in the garden with my glove. Perhaps someone had seen me in the window watching him. Hadn't I noticed a shadow at the window across from me, and hadn't the curtain there moved? It could be one of the household staff. But where would a servant get such fine stationery unless it had been stolen?

Above all, what did the message mean? If it was from Iris, or Werner, or one of the servants, why mention a horn? I linked the threat with my feelings for Maximillian. But perhaps these thoughts welled up from my own guilt about the way I had dreamed of the man. Maybe the note had nothing to do with him.

Confused and upset, unable to make any sense of the warning, I went down to Dr. Demel's office for the difficult session I had been so happy to postpone—the interview about my father's death.

"So you think the melancholic streak in your father contributed to his suicide?"

"Yes. Forces over which he had no control triggered it."

"What forces?"

"Envy."

"Whose?"

"His colleagues'."

"What did they do?"

"After his trip to Vienna he was devoting more and more time to treating patients whose problems had a strong emotional overlay. He was a society doctor. He had some money and began to set large portions of it aside for research."

"Lucky man."

"Yes. But he also worked hard and deserved the money."

"Of course."

"Anyway, his patients knew he started a research fund. They contributed to it. They were so enormously helped by him they wanted to show their appreciation. Some, to encourage his work, left considerable money for the fund in their wills. His modest resources grew."

"Was he going to establish his own clinic with the money?"

"Yes. And further his research."

"Where did you fit into the picture?"

My cheeks grew hot, and my heart began to pound from the deep frustration and raw anger I had never resolved. I gripped the sides of the armchair and leaned toward Demel, my voice harsh. "I was to finish medical school and be my father's partner."

"And continue the close relationship you had with him since your mother's death."

"We were a good team."

"I don't doubt it."

"Then why do you bring that up? Why focus on it?"

"Am I?" asked Demel.

"I think so."

Dr. Demel's knowing smile made me think he was reading my thoughts, and I felt uncomfortable.

"You don't have to apologize about your feelings toward your father. Most girls—"

"I'm not apologizing," I snapped.

Demel studied me through lazy-lidded eyes. When he watched me like that, he did not seem like a doctor. He did not look at me the way a friend of my father should. I was anxious to proceed with the interview, and then put it behind me.

"One extremely wealthy patient," I went on, "left a large amount to the Hopkins Foundation. There was enough seed money for my father to leave the Philadelphia Hospital and go out on his own."

"But he never did."

I shook my head.

"What happened, Emily? Tell me."

I remained silent. With shocking clarity I could see the ugly headlines. The dark ink stretched before my disbelieving eyes just as it did the morning I first saw the words. **DOCTOR POCKETS MONEY**.

"I can't go on," I whispered.

"You must," he replied. "You can't go forward in life unless you deal with the issues from the past."

"That's what I thought coming here to Vienna would do . . . but it's too painful."

"Your eyes are full of hurt, Emily. Purge yourself of it. I'll listen."

Demel's voice was low and compassionate. He was trying to help me, comfort me. I couldn't say exactly why, but I sensed he had some other reason for wanting me to talk about myself. I had this feeling before, but in my acute stress at present, I chose not to heed it.

"What are you afraid of?" he asked in soft, liquid tones. "Tell me, Emily. I knew you and your papa. I'm like your papa, am I not? You can talk to me," he soothed.

"Papa's colleagues accused him of stealing the money and putting it to his personal use," I continued shakily.

"Why?"

"They were jealous. Their patients never thought as well of them. They had hopes of convincing my father to use the fund for their pet projects in the hospital. Papa was wealthier than they. All these reasons," I said.

"How could they prove theft?"

"They altered the figures and went to the press."

Demel winced. "And then?"

"They knew my father was sensitive, that he couldn't take a lot of pressure, that he was, to some extent, naive. They knew how to get to him."

"How did they?"

"Through me."

In the silence that followed, those words ricocheted off the walls, battering me again and again until tears welled in my eyes.

Despite them, I went on, in half-strangled sounds. "The journalists had no conscience. They did nothing but dwell on the negative. With their nasty innuendos they made my father appear to be endangering the public. People start to believe what they read and hear if they see and hear it often enough."

Demel looked incredulous.

"But all this my father could have endured if he felt I believed him."

"Didn't you?"

"Yes."

"Well—"

"He wasn't told that. Don't forget, some of my professors at medical school were my father's colleagues. They told him they saw me daily and that I was coming out against him, though I fought with them and called them liars."

"Your father believed them?"

Anger and pain nearly closed my throat. I struggled to finish. "Papa and I had an argument at breakfast over something insignificant. The newspaper that day claimed to have new evidence in the case, damning allegations. And later that afternoon his enemies lied and told him I was on their side."

I paused, weeping quietly. Dr. Demel grasped my hand. "W-when I went h-home that night he . . . he was dead."

I felt as though I was kicked in the chest. Long minutes passed. "That's not all," I whispered when I had recovered enough to speak. "They forced me out of medicine."

"How?"

"They harassed me."

"Why?"

"Maybe because of their own guilt they didn't want to face me. I was a reminder of what they had done to a good man, a worthy physician."

"What did they do to you, Emily?"

"I hired a lawyer to look into the contract my father had with the hospital. The question was, what would happen to the funds? I wanted to carry on my father's work." I laughed harshly. "But his greedy colleagues wanted the money. They went on a hateful campaign to make me leave. Subtle hints, cruel asides. They tried to destroy my reputation. There are few female doctors, you know. I had no support in a male-dominated profession. I couldn't take it anymore and left."

"What happened to the money?"

"A clause in the trust fund reverted the money back to the hospital if it was not used for my father's clinic."

"Then you worked as a companion in Dr. Kirkbride's hospital?"

"Yes."

"My, my. What a thing to live through."

"That experience shaped my life. Those men ended two careers. They murdered my father and destroyed something in me."

Dr. Demel held my hand, slowly stroking my fingers. "What?" he asked smoothly.

"Trust."

"You don't trust anyone?"

"I'm careful. Ever since that time I've been cautious and highly sensitive to what's right and wrong. I've had to deal with my own guilt and fears."

"What fears?" Again the silken voice.

Later I was to wonder what sorcery Demel performed to get me to say it. I wondered how I could have ignored my own warnings and admitted my darkest terror.

"What are they, Emily?" His voice was cool, soothing.

"I was used," I bit out. "I think I would kill if I were to trust again and be betrayed."

Demel did not answer.

There was an insistent rap at the door, and he went to open it. The butler stood there, stiffly.

"Professor Doctor," the man said, "you're wanted in the clinic right away."

"I'll be there in a few minutes."

"It appears," he said woodenly, "you're needed immediately."

"Can I be of help?" I asked Demel.

"Thank you, but I won't be long. Meantime, take a little walk. It'll be good for you."

Gray clouds smeared the sky overhead. The paths beyond the gardens were in shadows, yet I could see a slim figure half crouched by a bench. Her head was down, and she pulled her cloak closely about herself.

She was stirring a small pile of leaves with a stick as I approached. "Frau Steinmetz," I called.

"Toil and trouble," she mumbled. "Toil and trouble."

"Frau Steinmetz, it's Emily Hopkins. I spoke with you yesterday."

Watery gray eyes turned to greet me. She shook her head. "You don't remember?"

"Trouble," she said wearily, "is all around us. The curse of God is what we'll get."

I helped her up, smiling. "What trouble?"

There was a palpable silence. The woman looked stricken. She moved wearily to sit on the bench. "The weight is all on me."

"The burden of your ill father?"

Fear touched her eyes. "D-don't ask."

The day was darkening; sooty clouds thickened in the sky and cast everything below in a sinister light. Naked branches of oak trees dipped somberly in a nervous wind. A bell from a distant church grimly tolled the hour with twelve mournful strokes.

Frau Steinmetz shivered.

I tried to console her. "There, there now. It's only the wind."

"Nay,'tis the voice of the devil," she replied.

"Now what would Dr. Schaller say to that, Frau Steinmetz?"

She stared unblinking at a twisted tree root by her foot. "He didn't come today."

I was surprised at this, and wondered if Maximillian was attending another lecture. If so, he had not mentioned his plans to me. *And why should he have?* I quickly chided myself.

"When did you see Dr. Schaller last?" I asked.

"Yesterday afternoon," she muttered.

"Well, I'm sure he'll be back soon," I said comfortingly, but the woman was inconsolable. She dug her fingernails into the palms of her hands. She kicked restlessly at the exposed tree root. Her face was a mask of worry and sadness.

"It's up to me," she whimpered.

I took her hands in mine. "We'll help you."

The wind swept through the bare branches with a low, hollow hum.

"Satan's song, *that* is."

Poor woman. She was worse today than yesterday, I realized. With a faraway look she spoke of the torment she suffered and asked me to visit her later. I promised her I would, and turned onto the footpath. Werner was there.

"You act like a lady doctor."

"Do you always eavesdrop?"

"When the conversation intrigues me."

"What about Frau Steinmetz could interest *you*?"

He flicked the ashes from the tip of his cigar. "She's been here for a while. I've gotten to know her and feel sorry for her."

Werner Demel *kind*? Now *I* was curious.

"It's easy to be sympathetic. She's a nice lady." He drew on his cigar. "You know, the more I see these people, the more I think they probably can't help the way they feel."

"What do you mean?"

"It's as if their minds are vulnerable and can't ward off something that's like an attack. I don't know how else to put it."

"Now *you're* playing the doctor," I said and laughed.

"Maybe." He shrugged. "Say, it looks like rain is coming. I've tried to convince Peter to go inside, but he won't listen."

"Where is he?"

"By the pond."

Shaggy pine boughs slapped and moaned in the gathering wind, brushing my cheek, then pressing close above my head.

The sound was a warning Frau Steinmetz said. Satan's song she'd called it. Poor thing was riddled with guilt.

Scuttling noises came from the shrubs, and a fleeting shadow darted ahead. I jumped back. "Peter?"

If there was an answer, it was swallowed by the wind. I took a steadying breath to still my budding fear. There was another noise now, a low snap behind me, and I whirled about, only to find the path dark and barren. "Peter!" I shouted.

Not the slightest sound came.

Again I sensed some movement in the bushes to my right. I turned with trembling hand to hold them back and face what I feared would be some demon-beast, so plagued was I by the old woman's thoughts.

Just then something white scooted in front of me, squawking loudly. "Herman," I exclaimed.

The duck stomped about, flapping its wings.

"Did he do something wrong, Miss Hopkins?"

I sagged with relief at Peter's voice. "He startled me, that's all."

"Are you angry?"

"No."

"Then why are you shouting?"

"I was looking for you. It's going to pour any minute. We should go inside."

"Can Herman come?"

"Is he allowed?"

The boy shook his head.

"Believe me, he won't mind getting wet."

"I want to show you something before we go." He crooked a finger. "Come here."

To the edge of the brook I went.

"Look down there." He pointed to a recessed rock with water flowing around it.

"My tutor and I are going to catch him and cook him in the grate by the shed."

"Really?"

"And then we're going to eat him. Just like before."

I was so pleased to hear this I barely felt the first few drops of rain.

I felt a tug at my sleeve. "It's raining now, Miss Hopkins."

"So it is." I laughed.

Hand in hand we ran back toward the mansion, and to my shock I saw Frau Steinmetz still sitting on the bench. "Run along, Peter. I'll help her inside."

So saying, I put my arm around her and got her to her feet. I looked heavenward, beseeching the clouds to hold their fury. And in this upward glance I saw the villa, a monstrous dark hulk against an angry sky. I saw a blackened door of wood, the patch of rough stucco, and I huddled close to the frail creature who was smiling strangely.

Once inside the clinic I learned what had upset the dear woman. The unit was alive with tension. What I did not know is that this world of madness would affect my life in sordid, hideous ways.

Fear and uncertainty were etched on the faces of the patients. The hospital staff seemed worried, especially Bertha. She marched from one room to the other, barking orders, then came to me.

"I'll take Frau Steinmetz."

"She's no problem. I know where her room is."

"I'll take her," the matron insisted.

"What's happened?"

"We don't need any interference. We can manage by ourselves. Now, if you'll excuse me," Bertha said crisply, "I'll get Frau Steinmetz settled."

Johann walked straight past me without speaking. He seemed in shock. Even Herr Baumer was subdued. He joined two other men who milled about, looking anxious.

One of the two glanced gravely toward Herr Kirsch's room and put his hands to his head. "Ach-h-h," he shrieked.

I followed the direction of that cry. Herr Kirsch's door was closed. I knocked. Once. Twice. And then I opened it and slipped inside.

Herr Kirsch looked stiff, waxen. I knew that moment he was dead.

I remembered how agitated and confused he was the previous evening, how he talked of taking over Demel's position. He was overactive, enthusiastic, even humorous, I recalled. Feeling sorry for the old man, I moved closer to him and noticed that his eyes were still open.

Footsteps in the hall grew louder. The door was pushed inward.

"What are you doing in here?" Bertha snapped.

"I wanted to find out what was wrong, to see if I could help."

"Go right out that door," she said, pointing. "That's how you can help. Dr. Demel wants anyone who doesn't belong to leave."

I did as asked, and saw Maximillian walking briskly in the hallway toward me.

"Have you heard?" I asked.

"Yes, the poor man. And while I was gone! It must be bedlam in there."

"Exactly," I said.

Despite his concern for what was happening in the clinic, he looked at me intently just then and smiled. "My family is going out tonight to the home of one of Iris' friends. I don't want to waste an evening listening to their mindless prattle. Will you join me for dinner?"

"Where?"

"In the parlor upstairs. At eight."

I nodded.

His smile deepened.

I flew to my room, delighted.

Hours later, I crossed the corridor to that parlor, wearing a gossamer confection of shimmering lemon silk. The skirt floated about me in rich clouds of gold, while the lacy bodice was form-fitting and low.

When I entered the room, Maximillian was standing by the fireplace, one hand on the mantel, the other cradling a glass of brandy. He was staring into the flames. Slowly he turned, a model of sartorial splendor in a claret smoking jacket that emphasized the magnificent sweep of his shoulders. His snowy shirtfront was studded with rubies, catching the light from the blaze. But even these gems could not match the glitter of appreciation in his deep blue eyes. He strode forward, holding out a hand, and a shiver of pleasure rippled through me.

It was apparent dinner was to be informal, private, and delicious. Luscious aromas wafted from the silver chafing dishes on the buffet. A small table was beautifully set near the cozy fire. Maximillian, ignoring all the trimmings for the moment, guided me to the settee and sat beside me.

"Will you have an aperitif?"

"A glass of sherry would be fine."

He reached for the crystal decanter on the rosewood table before us. Only then did I notice the strain on his face.

"It must have been difficult in the clinic this afternoon," I offered sympathetically.

"Awful," he replied, handing me my glass. "In part, I suppose, because it happened so close to the last one."

"The death, you mean."

"Yes. Two in a month."

"I remember," I answered grimly.

"And I was gone for both."

"Where were you?"

"In the tenements. Every Thursday I go there to do whatever I can for those people."

"Frau Steinmetz misses you when you're gone."

His brow furrowed. "How do you know that?"

"Yesterday I visited the hospital with Dr. Demel. I spoke with a couple of patients . . . Frau Steinmetz and Herr Kirsch."

Max's eyes widened with interest. "How was he when you saw him?"

"Not good. His thoughts were disordered. They streamed out of him rapidly. They were changing, disconnected."

Maximillian sighed. "He had a tendency to do that. He was elderly, you know. And insane."

"But he had physical complaints, too. He was thirsty and hot and dizzy."

"It's hard to sort out what's real and what's not in patients like him."

"You saw him after I did, according to Frau Steinmetz. She said you went to the clinic in the late afternoon. How did you find him?" I asked.

"It was evening, and Bertha told me he was sleeping. I looked into his room, and he was."

"Did she tell you he had felt ill earlier?"

"Come to think of it, no."

So engrossed were we in our conversation, I don't think either one of us noticed exactly when we moved to the table and started to eat. It was wonderful to talk about patients again, to compare notes. It all seemed so effortless. Max was easy to be with—too easy.

We dug into perfectly spiced red cabbage, delicate schnitzel, a tureen of pork with truffles, and all the while the conversation never stopped.

"It was a shock to the other patients," Max continued.

"So I discovered."

"Yes. These matters are usually discreetly managed. The person is taken away while the others are all at dinner or asleep."

I remembered the strange little room the night of my arrival, and asked, "Where was Herr Kirsch's body taken?"

"To a small alcove downstairs."

I felt goose bumps form at the thought of that windowless room, and I pursued a line of questioning without consciously knowing why. "Will there be a postmortem?"

"If the family wants it. But the Kirsches probably won't be any different from others who institutionalize relatives at great expense. Sadly, they are often relieved by the death and don't request an autopsy." Maximillian grew thoughtful. "I wish I hadn't been away yesterday or today. I feel I would have a better grasp of what's happened." He sat back in his chair and sighed. "Guilt is what I'm suffering from, Emily."

"You shouldn't. You have to keep abreast of developments in your field. What did Dr. Freud lecture about?"

"Hypnosis. And it was fascinating. When he hypnotizes his patients, they describe the circumstances that surround the development of their symptoms. Recalling these memories evokes the same powerful emotions they felt during the experience, but could not admit to. Afterward, Freud says, their symptoms are reduced or gone."

"Do you think the technique would work with Frau Steinmetz?"

"I doubt it. Freud uses it to treat hysteria, not melancholia. Frau Steinmetz can't tell herself she resents taking care of her father. If she did, she would think she's not a good woman, not a devout Christian, etcetera. She's terribly guilt-ridden."

"But not as much as you," I commented playfully, trying to lighten Max's mood.

He laughed at this, his eyes twinkling.

I took a long sip of wine. "Perhaps you'll need a hypnotist, or some such therapist, Dr. Schaller."

"I already have one," he replied, an odd tension in his voice.

Some reckless bent spurred me on. "Who?"

He set his glass down and studied me for an endless moment. "You," he said softly. "You have me in a trance."

Not expecting this strong admission, I flushed and looked away.

He reached across the table and turned my chin until my eyes again met his. "What am I going to do about you, Emily? Tell me."

To my shock, the door opened, and two servants stepped inside, their eyes showing embarrassment at the intimate scene. His hand fell. We sat back in our chairs. They cleared our dishes quickly and then placed a tray of scrumptious desserts before us. Then they left.

I was glad for the interruption, because I didn't know how to answer Maximillian. But I was also concerned that the footmen would gossip.

"What will it be, Emily, apple strudel, hazelnut macaroons, or sachertorte?"

"How about a little of each?"

"Strudel is Peter's favorite sweet. I hope they've saved him some," Max said. "That he'll eat."

"He eats other things."

"Like what? When? I feel as if I'm watching the boy starve to death."

I told Maximillian how I saw his son eating rolls in the kitchen and how he cooked and ate fish with his tutor.

"Do you think it's me, then?"

"What do you mean?"

"My fault. Am I pushing too hard and actually making him want to eat less, especially in front of me?"

"That could be. He likes to decide what he'll do and when he'll do it. Maybe he needs to feel he has control over this part of his life."

"God knows he must feel helpless about Iris' move to the Ringstrasse." There was a trace of sadness in his tone.

"Ease up on him," I quietly suggested.

"Thank you. I shall," Max replied appreciatively.

Once more our eyes met and held. Moments passed. In the space of the next tortured heartbeat, Maximillian got to his feet and brought me to mine.

His mouth crashed to my lips, cleaving to them, lingering upon them as if he loved the feel of them.

"Soft as silk," he whispered raggedly.

It was like my dream, but better than dreaming. Like make-believe, but sweeter than fantasy. More powerful, too, each stolen kiss long and heavy with heat, full of fury and reckless abandon.

With great reluctance Maximillian stepped back from me. "What's this? Tears, Emily?"

I blinked and brushed them away with my fingers. "I'm sorry."

"Don't be," he said gently, cradling my head in his hands. "Don't be sorry for us."

"Oh, Max, I'm afraid the servants will talk. Everyone will know."

With that, he strode to the door and flung it open. "See, no one." He looked down the corridor both ways and, taking my hand, stepped briskly across to my rooms. "To hell with them," he cried and swept me into his arms.

In the days ahead those precious moments with Maximillian would be my bulwark against the chilling and sinister forces into which I was being slowly and inexorably drawn.

✝ Chapter Nine

The mansion seemed swathed in silence the next day. No matter where I went, everything was quiet. The corridors were empty; no piles of linen, no chattering maids. One glance in the breakfast room made me want to return to my chamber and request a tray. Werner hid behind a newspaper. The sullen Dr. Demel hardly acknowledged me. Even the effusive Friedericke barely managed a hushed hello. I could not help but wonder what new gloom had descended upon the place. Had the servants' whispers reached them?

A chilling unease crept through me at the thought. I could still hear Max cursing the house staff's gossip. And then, blissfully, I could feel his arms about me, his lips upon mine.

But where would it end, this stolen pleasure? What would happen when the interviews for Papa's biography were over? Would I return to America pleased to have honored him, but heartbroken over the loss of Maximillian? It seemed so.

My somber mood soon matched that of this strange house. I had the uneasy feeling that the dark cloud hovering above us would thicken. I began to think about the clinic, the people and events there. And this brought me to the door of Demel's study early that afternoon.

He was in no mood to talk.

"What, Miss Hopkins?"

"I wanted to speak to you about the clinic."

"Be brief."

I sat down.

He looked at me curiously, wondering, no doubt, if I'd heard him.

I stayed seated anyway. "It's about Herr Kirsch."

"The matter is all taken care of. The family has been notified and the body removed."

"So fast?"

"It's best that way."

"But—"

"It's over. A dead issue, if you'll pardon the bad pun, Miss Hopkins."

"And Bertha?"

"What about her?"

"How long has she worked here?"

Dr. Demel got to his feet and stood over me. "Why so many questions?"

"How well do you know her?" I persisted.

"One rarely knows oneself, let alone someone else."

"She seemed so hostile yesterday."

"People don't always act appropriately when they're anxious."

I felt as if he were defending her and evading my questions. I wondered why. I was not quite sure where my queries were leading, but my host's answers intrigued me.

"Do you think Herr Kirsch was closely monitored?"

Demel went to the window, keeping his back toward me. "I had adequate staffing the night he died."

"How much coverage did you have?"

"Ask Maximillian. He makes up the schedule."

"Was Bertha on duty?"

He turned to me then, his tone cold. "What do you have against the woman? She does her job."

"But a death on the service should not be taken lightly." I wished I could have bitten back the words.

"Who says it is?"

"I'm sorry. I didn't mean to—"

His harsh voice soared over mine. "What *did* you mean?"

I didn't exactly know myself. I had come to Demel's study

wondering if Herr Kirsch's death could somehow have been prevented. I was frank, perhaps too direct. But Demel was fiercely defensive. I was beginning to wonder what, or whom, he was protecting.

"Answer me."

"I-I'm not sure."

His laughter had a sharp, deprecating edge to it. "You're what?"

At my shocked silence, Demel's tufted brows rose in indignation. I was witnessing a new facet of the man. Gone was yesterday's empathy and reason. Replacing them was anger, stark and scathing, fueled, I thought, by fear. *Of what?*

"You have come into my study, raising unnecessary questions, and you don't know why? May I remind you, Miss Hopkins, that the deceased was elderly and mentally ill. His symptoms, his physical complaints, and the way he expressed them to both of us were manifestations of his illness and age."

"How old was he?"

"Seventy-five."

Feeling chastened, I rose to leave. "My apologies, Dr. Demel."

His hands nervously patted back the waves in his hair. "They're accepted."

Halfway to the door I turned. "I guess you have nothing to worry about," I said, yet I was filled with lingering doubt. I paused and stared meaningfully at him, finding the right tone. "Do you?"

His expression was closed, unreadable, his voice a dark whisper. "Let it go, Miss Hopkins."

I didn't like his forbidding tone. It was beginning to remind me of another time and place where men lied to save themselves, when they deceived and threatened my father and me. With cold, bony fingers, fear squeezed my heart. Still, I faced him.

It was a long, measuring stare.

Again, the contemptuous mirth. "Do we understand one another?"

I nodded slowly.

"Good."

Again I meant to go, but his words stopped me.

"I have spent years running this sanitarium," he said warningly. "With your help, I had planned to improve it. Don't disappoint me."

Each mellow strike of the acorn clock pealed like thunder in my mind. Raw memories returned. I felt myself blanch. I saw Demel smile, a grin that mocked as cruelly as those others. He knew he was intimidating me, and the triumph in his eyes made me ill.

I had told him too much. Trusted him. Laid myself bare. He knew my weaknesses, could use them against me.

A strange gurgle rose in my throat, an unreal sound, soft and menacing, that welled up from the springs of hurt and hate. The noise twisted through my rage-tightened throat; it slid over my lips, a demented, hysterical laugh.

Demel appeared stunned.

I had to get out, leave this dreadful place. Go home. But not without a spiteful parting word. I don't know from where or how I got my courage. It was as though I could hear my father's anguished weeping, feel his despair.

"I'll do what I have to do," I spat, pivoting toward the door.

The room seemed to narrow with the tension.

I could feel the heat of Demel's eyes on my back. "Do anything stupid," he hissed, "and I'll write a scathing biography of your father and credit you with all the information in it."

"What you say won't be true," I cried. "It's blackmail."

Demel's laugh was bitter. And then, as casually as if he were flicking unwanted lint from his coat, he added, "I deceive less than I am deceived, Miss Hopkins."

I was sick with disgust. I was outraged. Slamming the door, I fled up the staircase, passing Iris who was standing by the large window on the landing.

"Ooo!" Her lips pursed distastefully. "What's the hurry?"

"Nothing."

She studied her fingertips. "Will I need an umbrella?"

"I don't know."

"Be a dear, tell me if it's raining."

"See for yourself," I snapped and ran down the hallway.

The next door to slam was mine.

Flooded with anger and sadness, I sank onto the bed. My mind reeled with the sound of Demel's voice, derisive and ugly, with the hateful meaning of his words, with his distorted and shameful ambitions. That's what was at the root of this. That's what had motivated my father's enemies.

In my mind's eye I saw those cruel men who had killed my father with the deliberateness and equanimity of a firing squad. Disgraced is what they said I would be. Dishonored, discredited. They forced me out of my profession and in my grief I could not stand against them. No, like some haunted, and hunted, piteous prey, I fled.

And Demel knew it! He got me to talk about myself when I told my father's life story. He seduced me into thinking my secrets were safe, that he was my protector as well as my father's advocate. And, now, to serve his own ends, he would use me.

As others had!

If I were not so sickened by this thought I might have laughed. There was some twisted irony in it, after all. I had come to Vienna to help clear my father's name. Instead, my testimony would damn him.

I was chuckling now, the hideous giggle that bubbled from my throat in Demel's study. I was crying, too. How idealistic I had been. How innocent. How cursed I felt to be twice the fool!

Hadn't I learned?

Waves of anger and fear continued to wash over me. Clearly Demel was not the man he appeared to be. He was a chameleon, changing at will to suit any situation. At times, charming and expansive; at others, moody and withdrawn. He'd been kind, protective like a father, and the next day forbidding and threatening. He was a sum of contradictions. I wondered now what he would do.

My thoughts kept returning to the clinic. What really had happened there? I had thought Herr Kirsch's death might have resulted from carelessness. Tragically, oversights happen. But Demel's response to my questions was as swift and sharp as an avenging sword. Of what was he fearful?

Two deaths in the weeks I had been here. I knew nothing of the circumstances surrounding the first. Should I probe? Demel had forewarned me. If I did not drop the matter, I would painfully regret it. I had buckled under such a threat once before. Would I again, now that the stakes were higher?

With new resolve, I moved to the dressing table to repair my appearance. The woman in the mirror looked different; the expression in her eyes was self-assured, her chin more determined, her lips curled slightly in a secretive smile.

I would stop working with Demel on the biography. I would go to the clinic, become a vigilant observer of everyone and everything there. No one would know of my plans. Not even Demel would suspect, for I would fool him.

There was a knock at the door.

"Come in," I called. Even my voice had a new ring of certainty.

"Just me, miss," answered Hannelore. "Oh," she exclaimed, seeing me remove the combs in my hair, "let me help."

"Do something," I implored. "I want a different hairdo."

"You have such nice hair," Hannelore went on, running her fingers through its waves.

"There's lots of it. That much I'll agree to."

"So shiny. Burnished red on brown. I'd love to have it."

"I warn you. It can be stubborn."

"Not in my hands."

Her fingers worked with the artistry of a harpist. Sweeping the hair from my face, parting it, forming a loosely woven chignon, she smiled with satisfaction when she placed the last mother-of-pearl hairpin in place. "There. Do you like it?"

Studying my reflection, I replied, "Very much."

So much, I hardly noticed the maid's departure. Staring at me was a new person. But I wondered with the next breath how far beneath the surface was the old. Demel would be a formidable opponent if I defied him. I had caved in to threats before. I had become thin-skinned, overly sensitive to gossip and criticism. Now I had emerged from that dark tunnel with black-and-white vision, and a clear-cut sense of right and wrong.

Demel's behavior was reprehensible.

Is yours any better? a small voice asked.

I couldn't say. I wasn't sure. I only knew I had fallen in love with a man who was legally and rightfully married. Did that make me as "bad" as Demel?

The face in the mirror had no answer.

Some thin thread of sound penetrated these thoughts, a whisper so faint I thought it mine. A flash of movement in the reflecting glass drew my attention, and I turned to the door. Did it move slightly? I turned into the dim hallway just in time to see a dark form slip around the corner at the far end. The hairs on my arms stood up straight. Who had been watching me?

Snatching up my cloak, I followed that elusive being. The hall led to the main staircase, but by the time I reached it, there was no sign of anyone. Annoyed, I waited a few moments, then went outside to the woodland path.

Two brownish-red squirrels gathering walnuts stood in my path. As I approached, one ran behind a tree stump, while the other, without so much as a questioning glance at me, sat on his haunches, arched his fluffy tail, and licked his prize. I moved on.

I skirted the duck pond and wandered down a steep sloping meadow. Nestled in its base was a cottage where asters bloomed riotously in the garden amidst kraut and salad greens. Lace curtains graced the windows, and smoke curled from the chimney. I walked past the woodpile, prudently stacked for the winter ahead, past the water trough for the animals, past all the signs of peaceful, happy lives. I tried not to compare mine with these, but I could not stop thinking of Maximillian, Peter, and living with them in a home so lovingly tended.

To shake these thoughts, I quickened my pace and headed back to the house.

Despite my vigorous strides, Werner caught up with me. His dark coat was neatly tailored, his shirt fresh, his smile wide.

"Why the rush?"

"I'm upset," I replied, still walking.

"Who wouldn't be."

I didn't know what he meant, and when I turned to him, puzzled, he explained. "I heard you fighting with Onkel Franz."

I could only stare at him, my bottom lip between my teeth.

"Don't worry," he said reassuringly. "I won't tell anyone."

If I had to choose one person whom I would not want to know the details of that argument, it would be Werner. No, maybe Iris, I amended. "What did you hear?"

"I heard you scream 'blackmail.' "

"Do you know why?"

"Yes."

I groaned.

"Cheer up," he said. "I can help."

"How?"

Werner paused to take a thoughtful puff of his cigar. He blew out a long, thin stream of smoke, then turned toward me. "I have a friend who's a journalist. I could have him come talk to you."

I almost gagged. "A journalist is the last person I'd want to see."

"Why?"

"Never mind." I started to move on.

"Look," Werner said, touching my shoulder. "I know we got off on the wrong foot, you and I, but I'd like to rectify that."

I was surprised. The man had given me every reason not to trust him, yet he nonetheless seemed to want to make amends. His behavior had improved since our first meeting. He'd been kind to Frau Steinmetz. Perhaps he had been considerate of me when he read me the personal ads. Maybe he had not been threatening to put anything in the newspaper about Max and me, but warning me instead that others might do this.

I was curious. Why would he want to expose a possible scandal at the house where he lived and worked? Perhaps he could provide me with some answers.

"How many patients have died at the asylum?"

"In the last few years, several."

"Does that surprise you?"

"It's not so unusual."

"When was the last death?"

"The night you arrived."

"Were you, or anyone else, troubled by it?"

"Not really. The woman was elderly."

I wondered now if I had overreacted to Herr Kirsch's death and to Demel's response to it. Had I read more into his actions than was there? But if I was wrong about them, why would he try to blackmail me? I started to frown.

"You worry too much," Werner said.

"How can I not after what your uncle said?"

"You don't know my uncle."

"Explain him to me then."

"The census is low. So is his capital. I know because I keep the books. He needs more patients or he'll go under. Add this to his pathological fear of bad publicity, and you'll realize the man feels his back is to the wall."

I thought there was more to the story than this explanation. I had spent several weeks being interviewed by Demel. He was a man of many moods, of high emotions. None were shallow. I witnessed the anger and panic in his face when I spoke of Bertha and Herr Kirsch. I looked at Werner quizzically.

He laughed as if he was truly amused. What did he find so funny? I felt he did not understand my situation—and I did not understand his. If the sanitarium was in financial trouble, why would he want this and other problems revealed? My mind kept going back to that point.

"Why would you want the press nosing around here?" I asked.

Werner took the cigar from his mouth and stared at the length of gray ash at its tip. He looked away from me. "I've wanted to sell this place for years," he said without a trace of emotion.

I was startled.

He flicked off the ashes and laughed again. "Poor Emily, so pure of heart, so unsure of what you've come to here."

I did not like the way he was teasing me, and I tried to steer the conversation away from me and toward other concerns.

"How long has Bertha worked in the clinic?"

"Forever."

"Does she have any say in its operation?"

"Too much, sometimes."

"Meaning . . . ?"

"I think she has something on my uncle. I don't know what. I have little to do with her, and prefer to keep it that way."

Another dead end, I thought. Just like the one up ahead on our footpath. We turned into a branching path to the left and walked in silence for a while.

When we returned to the mansion, I said, "Don't contact your friend. It may not be necessary."

He nodded and went inside.

I took a different door, one leading to the clinic.

Demel and Maximillian stood by the window, talking. Their faces were silhouetted by late afternoon sunlight that poured through the glass. I could not see Demel's expression clearly when he became aware of my presence, but there was no denying the surprise and concern in his voice.

"May we help you, Miss Hopkins?"

"Perhaps *she* can help *us*," Max corrected.

Demel appeared to frown.

"Really," Max continued, "if Bertha can't be here tonight, Miss Hopkins could easily fill in."

"I would be glad to," I offered, pleased to have a bona fide reason to be near the patients.

Demel didn't miss a beat. "Of course," he exclaimed, "why didn't I think of it!"

Walking toward me, Maximillian explained, "I'm off tonight, but Dr. Demel is on duty. If you have any questions, he'll answer them."

"Naturally," Demel responded again. "In fact, Miss Hopkins, why not come to my study right after dinner so we can go over the procedures?"

I nodded warily, wondering why the man feigned eagerness for me to be in the clinic.

The thought preyed on my mind when I went upstairs; it lingered after my nap. But while I ate, I dismissed it. What could he do to me? I had to concentrate on my own plan of action which would make me privy to the inner workings of the asylum.

At eight o'clock, Demel opened his door to me. "Goodness," he said with a smile, "you're early. Come in, come in, we have time for a glass of sherry."

"Heavens, no," I demurred. "Not when I'm about to go to work."

"Coffee, then?"

"Yes, that would be fine."

The room felt warm and welcoming. A fire blazed cheerfully, casting mellow lights upon the wooden floor, softening the dark furniture, as well as the unsightly stacks of papers and supplies.

Demel went to the bookcase and poured himself a brandy. Lifting the silver coffeepot from a small table, he filled two cups.

"Sugar?"

"Three. I like it sweet."

There was no economy of motion on Demel's part. He dumped the brandy from the snifter into his coffee cup, splashing the liquid into the saucer. Several times he sprinkled sugar into my cup with an affable flair. When I smiled and turned away, I heard him hum. Later I regretted not watching those busy hands, but at the moment I was grateful for his carefree mood. He joined me by the fire with an expansive sigh.

"Ahh, the perfect cognac. *Wunderbar*."

I watched his tongue slide appreciatively over his lips. "If it's that special, why put it in your coffee?" I asked.

"Try some. You'll see."

"No." I shook my head. "I really shouldn't."

Holding his forefinger and thumb a wee bit apart, he winked. "This much?"

"Well, perhaps."

Demel started to pour the cognac straight from the bottle.

"Just a taste," I cautioned.

"A mouthful," he assured me.

The flames licked mercilessly at the aged wood, setting off wild sparks and cracks. Mesmerized by the fire's intensity, I sipped quietly at my drink.

"Well, what do you think?"

The coffee was sweet, much too sweet even for me, yet it had a strong aftertaste. "What kind of coffee is this?"

"Turkish and Colombian. Marvelous, isn't it?"

I did not want to dampen the man's mood. We were getting along nicely. So I agreed, taking several more sips, attributing the slight bitterness to the liquor as well as the blend of strong beans.

"When does the night shift start?" I asked, getting to the reason for my being here.

"In a little while," Demel said.

An odd reply, I thought. So unspecific.

"We should discuss the clinic procedures," I began again, but my voice seemed distant, strangely hollow.

Demel's answer was robust. "Absolutely."

Too loud, I thought, putting a hand over my ear. The man sounded as if he were inside my head.

The flames looked strange. They were blurred, pulsing savagely—like the rapid beating of my heart. I turned to Demel. "What's in this coffee? What are you doing to me? You snake!"

"Me?" he said sardonically, that derisive smile at the high corners of his mouth. "What about you? You know who's waiting in the room next door. *The press!* You sent the press here!"

I did not not quite get his meaning. I was frightened by the rush of a drug as it traveled through me. My legs began to fill with heaviness. As my fear intensified, my hands shook, rattling the cup in its saucer.

"What did you give me?" I screamed.

"Something we keep on hand here to calm the patients," he said.

"What? How much?"

"A minimal dose, a mere grain or—"

I flung the china at him, the last of the coffee spreading darkly on his shirt, the porcelain shattering on the floor.

With the patience of an artist, he dabbed a handkerchief at the stain. "Such temper," he chided. "Really, Miss Hopkins, you shock me."

I was enraged by his taunts, terrified of this unknown drug, but I had enough control to curse him. "You serpent! You slithering limb of Satan! No, Dr. Demel," I said, my lips working stiffly, fighting the dryness in my mouth, "you *are* the Devil himself . . . a fiend . . . a fraud."

He took an angry stride toward me, grabbing my shoulder. "You should talk," he spat.

"Let go of me," I shouted.

Again, that derisive laugh. "Soon you'll need me to stand up. In time you might be delirious, in a stupor. You'll begin to look like someone from the other wing."

I struggled to free myself, but I fell to the floor.

"What do you want from me? Why did you ever ask me here?"

"I've waited a long time for this clinic to be successful, but it's floundering. I need your knowledge of your father's methods. I hope to be famous, but events are conspiring against me, Miss Hopkins. Things are going wrong. I don't need your meddling to compound the mystery."

The door opened.

I watched four legs cross the carpet. *Was my vision that blurry?*

"Herr Aschoff," I heard announced above me. *"Die Presse."*

The press? I tried to scramble to my feet. Demel bent to help me. Keeping his back to the gentleman, he put his mouth to my ear. "How dare you!" he hissed.

He picked me up as if I were some bedraggled kitten. Then he spoke with a warmth and empathy that was loathsome. "Herr Aschoff, a moment longer, please. This poor patient has lost her way. She belongs in the asylum."

I watched the journalist look with dawning realization at the smashed china and at the stain on Demel's chest.

The men shared a knowing smile that filled me with disgust.

✝ Chapter Ten

The sun streamed through the windows, bathing my room in shafts of warm golden light. I put a hand to my eyes to block out the brightness.

"Ah, miss, you're finally awake."

I heard Hannelore's voice, but I couldn't answer her. My throat was parched, my mouth like cotton, and when I tried to raise my shoulders, my woozy head weighed me down like a bulky rock.

"I've been here the night, worried sick," she said.

I could barely nod.

"Dr. Demel asked me to stay," she added, fluffing the down *decke,* rearranging it to cover my feet.

Nausea rippled through me at the odious name, but I was curious about the man's request. "Wha-t?" I croaked.

" 'Tis fine," the maid went on sympathetically. "Happens to everyone." She bent closer, whispering, " 'Twas our own home brew that got you, was it?"

So he told her I was drunk.

"Lor', I never seen your eyes so bright. Like moons, they were."

My mind struggled to organize this information. I didn't respond.

But the good-natured girl didn't seem to mind the one-sided conversation. "I was frettin' somethin' fierce. What a relief you're all right. Now you take care," she said, patting my leg. "I'll be back with some food."

There wasn't a sign of Hannelore for a good long while, and during the wait I slowly came to, playing the events of the previous evening over and over in my brain.

Why did Demel do it? To keep me out of the clinic? To keep me from talking? From meddling, he'd said. In what? What was he afraid of?

The press!

Did Werner send Aschoff—after I asked him not to? Or was his appearance a coincidence?

Was Demel my only enemy? Was Werner my second? Were the two in cahoots?

I had no answers, only more questions, and they mushroomed in my mind like dark, avenging clouds.

I closed my eyes to rest again, but peace eluded me, for images of the baroque mansion stole under my eyelids and grew monstrously, spreading over me, smothering me like a ton of sand.

How could I win? How could I do what I came here to do?

The breeze that swayed the fringe of the draperies was cool and crisp. It brushed my cheeks refreshingly, felt good on my brow. I slowly sat up removed my fingers from my temples, and inhaled deeply.

"A good idea," Hannelore spoke soothingly. Setting down a tray, she moved to the window and pushed it full open. "Fresh air and strong coffee will fix you right."

"And a nice bath," I added.

"Right away."

I looked at the coffee and winced, doubting I could put it to my lips.

"Somethin' wrong, miss?"

"If it's not too much trouble," I said, putting an arm into the sleeve of my dressing gown, "I'd prefer tea."

The maid didn't hesitate. "All right," she said cheerfully.

I drew the bathwater myself and was soaking in it when she returned.

"Tell me about last night, Hannelore. I've never been-er-drunk before. Was I acting funny?"

Her face grew serious, her eyes as big as saucers. "Nay, miss, you was real strange. Scared, too."

"What did I do?"

"Couldn't see straight and acted"—she lowered her head, embarrassed—"if you'll pardon me, like-ah-"

"You can say it."

"Like you was d-dumb or somethin'. Not like yourself," she quickly added.

"Dazed?"

She snapped her fingers. "That's it."

"And Dr. Demel told you to bring me up here?"

"Gosh, yes. He was so worried 'bout you he made me stay the night in your room."

The oily skunk. He always could make himself look good. Even to Herr Aschoff he appeared the ever patient and understanding physician. A model of kindness.

"Did anyone else see me? I mean, was anyone, like . . . um . . . Dr. Schaller, aware of my condition?"

Thinking she understood, a smile lit her eyes. "Not to worry, miss. He never saw a thing. Dr. Demel and I scooted you up here fast as we could."

"Thank you, Hannelore."

"I like you, miss. I'd do it again." Still smiling, she brought me the tea and quickly left.

Despite the sweet-smelling water, its heat, or the warmth of the tea, I couldn't relax. My thoughts went back to the ugliness of the previous night, to Demel's mirthless laugh, to his malignant taunts and threats, to the heaviness in my limbs, to my confusion, the horror of the poison working its venomous way through me—all because he thought I was interfering in his clinic, the very place where he sought my help. The man ought to be locked up.

And he would be someday, if I had my way. But that time was far off. I had to think of the present and what I should do . . . if I should even stay here. I could have been killed. Murdered!

There, again, the sly snake knew what he was doing. Not much, a mere grain—as he silkily put it—just enough to put me under, to make me look, to an untrained eye, like one of his patients.

I feared Dr. Demel now, this man of extremes who made good his threats. But this last incident proved he, too, was afraid—afraid of me.

I closed my eyes. *What to do?*

"That's some long soak you're havin'."

"I can't help it, Hannelore," I mumbled.

She placed a hand on my shoulder. "Stay. I was only checkin' on you."

"No, it's time to get out."

I was grateful for her help, for her placid, nonjudgmental nature, and because of it I decided to ask more questions.

"I'm so embarrassed," I said, assuming a confessional tone. "What kind of liquor did I drink?"

"What we make ourselves." She nudged me playfully. "Strong, ain't it?"

"And what was I like? Tell me again."

"You was very thirsty."

"Did I drink much water?"

"Nay, miss, you was afraid to swallow."

That surprised me. "Was I afraid, or did I have difficulty swallowing?"

My pointed question made Hannelore look puzzled and a little hurt. "Gee, I dunno. I was just tryin' to take care of you."

"Of course. I'm sorry," I replied. "I guess I'm still upset."

The maid smiled sheepishly, then whispered, "I won't tell anybody you overdid it, miss. You have my word."

"Thank you," I said simply and proceeded to dress.

I didn't really want to know about the house brew. Demel gave me brandy. I only mentioned the liquor as a way of easing into questions about my behavior, for that knowledge would give me some idea of the drug Demel gave me—the drug that could be killing his patients.

When Hannelore felt she had mothered me enough and that I could be on my own, she excused herself. Soon after, cloak in hand, I went downstairs and found the family, without Dr. Demel, having afternoon coffee and cake.

"He has that duck in his room against my rules," Iris was saying. "The door is locked, and he won't open it." She looked at her husband expectantly, but Maximillian continued to study the platters of honey cake, strudel, and fruit tarts. "Are you listening, Max?"

Maximillian stared at his wife blankly. "No."

"Well, please do," she said, irritated. "It concerns *your* son."

I watched Friedericke nod to a footman who then placed still another dessert on the table.

"Ah!" exclaimed Max, "that's what I've been waiting for, red currants in that frothy meringue the cook whips up."

Iris grew flushed. "Do you want that stupid animal messing in the child's room? It's so unsanitary. The thought makes me sick."

"Well, please excuse yourself," Max replied. "You'll spoil our appetites."

Iris pushed her chair from the table and threw down her napkin. "Of all the insufferable—"

"Now, now," Friedericke counseled, patting her niece's arm sympathetically. "I'm sure Maximillian is only trying to tell you these matters are best discussed privately, not in front of guests." She smiled up at me. Heads swiveled.

"Join us, Miss Hopkins." Werner's tone was bright.

Max quickly rose and pulled out the chair next to him. "Please do."

Iris glared.

Peter stood in the doorway.

"I want to talk to you, young man," Iris said sharply.

Maximillian's mouth quirked. "Let him eat first."

The boy looked hesitant; he obviously did not want to sit down. "May I take a piece to my room, Papa?"

"Of course," Max replied. "Which one?"

Peter pointed to the strudel. "That."

"I'm not surprised," said his father, cutting off a generous slice.

Plate in hand, the child fairly skipped from the room, and when he was barely out of earshot, Iris warned her husband. "He's going to feed it to that damn duck and make more of a mess."

Max turned to her indifferently. "Will you have to clean it up?"

"Of course not."

"I'll have Peter do it himself, assuming there are a few crumbs. He's old enough."

"You'll do no such thing! We have servants."

Maximillian stared at her coldly. "Then what's really bothering you, Iris?"

"That he's disobeying me. That he's skinny as a rail. As ugly as some wretched foundling. God," she went on scathingly, "don't you realize in a couple of months we'll have to take him to Christmas parties looking like this?"

"Goodness," replied Maximillian, his voice dripping sarcasm, "whatever will people think?"

"Exactly!"

A muscle twitched in Maximillian's cheek. "Pity your son will embarrass you," he snapped. He added bitterly, "Your image is *so much* more important than his health."

"You're a doctor! *You* treat him!"

"Stop!" shrieked Friedericke, visibly upset. "You're making the rest of us terribly uncomfortable."

Everyone stared at her pink, quivering jowls, then quickly bent to their food. The conversation that followed was stilted, but I learned from it that the family, including me, was invited to a soirée at a friend's home the following evening.

When Friedericke got up to leave, the others followed. Wanting only to speak with Maximillian, I lagged behind, but he must have thought better of staying to talk with me. He gave me an apologetic smile and went on his way.

To pass time, I went to the breakfast nook and picked up a

magazine from the window sill. Voices came from the hall, and I looked up to see Iris sweep by without as much as a glance inside the room.

"Just a minute, young man."

"What, Mama?"

"I want to talk to you."

Though I turned the pages slowly, the print fluttered meaninglessly before my eyes.

"You had Herman in your room, didn't you?"

There was no reply.

"Answer me."

"M-maybe."

"No maybes. Did you or did you not have that animal in your room?"

"Y-y-yes."

"And you fed him your cake, instead of eating it. Am I right?"

"I-I—"

"Admit it. I know you did."

Iris' voice had a mocking self-satisfied edge to it, and my heart went out to the poor child who had to endure her dreadful tongue-lashing.

"S-sorry, Mama."

"Why don't you eat, Peter? You're looking frightful these days. Even Papa says you're scrawny."

Hearing that lie, I got to my feet and moved quietly to the door. I stood behind it, closing it slightly. The boy looked terrified.

"C-can't help it. N-not hungry," he answered in a reedy little voice.

"Why?"

Silence, save for the quickening of my heart.

"Answer me, dammit!"

Eyes cast downward, Peter bit his lip. "Dunno," he mumbled.

Enraged, Iris took a menacing step toward her son. She grabbed his jacket and jerked his frail body forward. "If I have to, I'll force you to eat. I'll stuff the food down your throat myself!"

The boy gasped, horrified. "I'll vomit." He spoke without artifice, I knew, for that was the fear he'd expressed in his nightmare, but Iris took it as defiance. I watched the long nails of her left hand dig into his shoulder. I saw, with horror, her right hand swing back and smack the child hard across the face.

"The sight of you sickens me!" she cried, throwing him from her. She twisted around and stormed off.

I dashed to the hall. "Peter!"

The child turned a helpless face to me, then looked away in shame. I held out my arms, whispering his name. He flew to me, hot tears flowing down his cheeks.

When his body stopped shaking, I told him I'd read to him. He nodded appreciatively. "You're good to me." He sobbed again.

"Hush, now," I soothed him, "when you're hungry you'll eat. It'll happen naturally. You'll see."

He brightened some, hugging me tighter. "I hope," he answered pitifully.

"Promise me you won't worry about eating?"

He nodded meekly.

"Now go clean up your room, and we'll catch up with each other later," I said, stroking his arm.

Visibly relieved, the boy smiled tentatively, gave me a little kiss, and ran to climb the servants' stairs.

I retrieved my cloak and went outside for some needed fresh air. Iris' vicious assault on her son, coming hard on the heels of my own terrifying experience with Dr. Demel, filled me with angry revulsion and sharp misgivings.

A raven dipped and wheeled in the sky, then swooped menacingly near my face. I put up my hands and shrank back, fearful now.

What to do? The thought returned to plague me. I hadn't seen Demel all day. Should I go to him, confront him again? I didn't know if I could. My mind kept going back to the last scene in his study, replaying his words: " . . . waited for this clinic to be successful . . . things are going wrong . . . your meddling compounds the mystery . . . a little something we keep on hand . . . you might be delirious . . . one of our patients lost her way."

Hannelore's voice joined his. "Miss, you was strange . . . eyes bright as moons . . . d-dumb . . . wouldn't swallow . . ."

I recalled my dry mouth and blurry vision. From atropine?

"Scary you was . . . eyes shining."

So were Herr Kirsch's! The life had gone out of his eyes, but they'd appeared glazed.

But why would Dr. Demel want to kill his patient, especially if he was worried about the reputation of his sanitarium? It made no sense.

Neither did Werner, who had been the first to tell me the hospital was in financial trouble. I had asked him not to contact his journalist friend. Had he? Or did the press already have wind of what was going on here and appear on their own?

"Damn duck, stomping my flowers." The voice was Friedericke's. She'd stepped outside and was holding Herman away from her, scolding him. A loud protesting squawk escaped the pet. I watched the woman put him to the ground. I saw her small black boot slip out from her voluminous skirts and swiftly kick the animal.

Herman shuffled his wide feet and snorted.

"Stay out here where you belong, or you'll next deal with me."

The duck squared his shoulders, fluffed his feathers, and marched to her, defiant.

She wagged a jeweled finger. "I'm warning you, and not for the first time, either."

Herman made a soft clucking sound and then with great dignity, he turned his back to Friedericke, stuck his tail high in the air and wiggled it furiously.

I smiled, despite my upset state of mind, returned to my ruminations, and decided that I should really speak to Werner.

But I didn't see the man again until the members of the Demel family and I were boarding the carriages for the soirée. Demel, Maximillian, and Iris rode in one coach; Friedericke,

Werner, and I, in another. It would have been inappropriate to broach the subject even if Friedericke had not monopolized the conversation. Her chatter was constant, much to Werner's delight.

Her eyes were glowing, giving her a rejuvenated, fresh appearance. "Look!" she exclaimed. "Did you ever see a more gorgeous brougham?"

"It belongs to the Wentzes," Werner replied, chuckling.

"I've never seen the like," Friedericke whispered.

Curious, I peered through the window and watched a handsomely finished gilded coach with numerous lamps pass us. Gold plumes adorned the horses' heads. Garlands of white flowers draped the vehicle's doors. Like a flash in the night, it streaked proudly ahead, while sidewalk on-lookers jostled one another and gaped.

Ours joined the parade of highly lacquered carriages that rolled to the door of the gaily lighted mansion. Liveried servants hastened to usher the guests inside. But once there, I quickly realized I did not belong. Clusters of stylishly gowned matrons and their husbands crowded the foyer, their knots of conversation filling the air. Hardly a face did I recognize, but those that I did, upon seeing my bewildered look, turned quickly from me.

"Not the most welcoming group, is it?" a husky, familiar voice whispered in my ear.

"I should have stayed home, Max."

"Nonsense. Stay by us, and I'll do what I can to help you."

During the performance I sat next to Werner, and he, thank heaven, put me at ease. At every pause in the musical program, he spoke so attentively to me I could not in my wildest imaginings picture him contacting Herr Aschoff of *Die Presse* against my wishes.

"It takes a while for these people to warm up to those they don't know," Werner confided.

"Strange custom, if you ask me."

"Act a little arrogant, and they'll come around faster."

"They'll think I'm someone important then?"

"Now you're catching on."

Listening to the musicians play Brahms and Bruckner, I began to leave all my cares behind me and relax. The performance was superb, and the applause showed it.

Everyone seemed saddened when the program was over. And then, as if it was spontaneous, the host announced a waltz contest. We were told to wait in the adjoining drawing rooms while the floor was cleared for dancing. Each guest would be given a card with numbers for each of several dances. Those who had matching numbers would be partners for that dance.

I could see Dr. Demel making his way toward me, and I hoped with all my heart I wouldn't have to dance with him.

"Miss Hopkins," he called, reaching for my arm, "are we to waltz?"

I turned just enough to make his fingers grasp air. "It depends on your numbers," I replied coolly. "What are they?"

He rattled them off.

I gave him my widest smile. "Sorry."

"I protest," he blustered with a long-suffering look.

"Tell that to the judges." I chuckled, moving away.

Werner and I were among the first few couples to dance. And with the floor almost empty, the room appeared to rival a king's. Ceilings and walls were conspicuously covered with intricate arches, mirrors, ornately carved moldings, Baroque angels, flowers, and vines, all richly detailed and gilded. They became a swirl of gold as we circled the room. Though my partner was a talented waltzer, executing smooth, even strides and graceful turns, I could tell we were outdanced by the other contestants.

My number was not called for the next dance, but Iris' was. Alluringly gowned in crimson silk, she was breathtakingly beautiful. As she glided on the floor, her bearing regal, there was a murmur of approval, an expectant hush. With a coy smile, she placed a gloved hand on her partner's shoulder. His arm reached around her delicate back. The music swelled.

The couple swayed. A sigh rose from the crowd.

Whether it was her partner's fault or Iris' I could not say; but instead of feeling the music and flowing with it, their steps were cautious, stiff, too precise. Iris' seductive smile dimmed; her face grew red. I swore I saw her grind her teeth. Then, to the shocked horror of all assembled, she began to lead while he, like some twitching marionette, followed.

It was an uninspired performance, well attested to by the embarrassed throat clearing and meager applause that followed.

"The final dance," the host announced. He listed the numbers.

It was my assigned number, and without looking up I knew it was Maximillian's. From where he stood, I sensed the heated glow in his eyes, the satisfied smile playing about his mobile mouth. Completely at ease, he walked over and offered me his arm. I placed my hand upon it graciously, my heart swelling with anticipation and pride. Then, for all the world as if we had been born there, we were in each other's arms, two hearts beating as one. I smiled into those intense blue eyes. They blazed back a message of confidence and trust. In the next moment we gave ourselves up completely to the glorious music.

It was pure heaven, paradise found. Maximillian waltzed divinely. With the sure touch of his hand low on my back, the solid strength of his leg against my skirts, he moved me round and round the ballroom.

Though filled with the excitement of the dance and its haunting, sweet rapture, I could not help but notice Iris' hot glare as we spun by her. I thought of the way she berated her husband, how she abused his patients, and struck her son, and I felt no sting of guilt or crumb of pity for her.

Other dancers began to ease their way to the edge of the crowd, leaving the floor to us alone. On we swirled in joyous abandon. Past the stares and furtive glances we whirled, past the twitters and snide asides, past the eyes above raised fans. Maximillian chuckled huskily, defying them all. The waltz,

Vienna's symbol of frivolity, gave us a measure of delirious freedom, and as the music built to its final crescendo, we let ourselves soar.

The applause was deafening.

"You are smooth," I whispered in Max's ear.

"You are my angel," he whispered back.

Next thing I knew, the host announced our names and handed me an armful of roses.

Careful of their delicate petals, I cradled the bouquet on the way to my bedchamber. To me, the musical evening was a smashing success, and all the way upstairs I hummed "Tales From the Vienna Woods," the piece Max and I had danced to.

There was no light on the second floor. Strange, I thought. I paused, wondering if I could find my room. Then I heard a whispery noise, a soft rustle. I clutched the railing and was just deciding to turn and go back down for a lamp when someone brushed my arm, then grabbed it.

"Don't move."

I gasped.

"Don't you move an inch until you tell me what you thought you were doing with *my* husband tonight."

"Waltzing," I replied.

Her nails bit into my arm. "Right under my nose."

"We didn't set the rules."

"Under my nose," she repeated, "for all to see."

I yanked my arm free. "When I think of what I've heard you do in the clinic, right under your husband's nose, I'd say this is a case of the pot calling the kettle black."

Her tone was cold with insult and fury. "You'll pay for this," she bit out. "Watch your back, for you'll dearly pay." With a gloating laugh, she moved swiftly away, her skirts trailing the steps in dark whispers.

✝ Chapter Eleven

I slipped into bed that night, chilled by Iris' threat—one more danger in this house of promised evil. My mind churned with anguished thoughts and fervent wishes. I longed for peace, but sound sleep was elusive despite the scent of roses and memories of Max waltzing with me in his swallow-tail coat.

Then, from the depth of night it came, a sob as tortured as my own.

"Papa."

A moment of hollow silence passed while I stared into the darkness of my room, my drowsy mind searching for time and place.

"H-help me." The pitiful cry sounded closer.

With trembling hand, I threw off the bed covers and hurried to the door.

"No . . . d-don't." The pleading voice was louder, more frenzied.

Heedless of my dress, I jerked the door open and found Peter outside my room, huddled miserably against the wall of the shadowed hallway. His arms flew up to his face when he saw me.

"Don't hit me . . . p-please," he whimpered.

I did not try to embrace him for fear he would not understand the meaning of my touch. "It's Emily. Open your eyes, Peter. Look and see."

"No, I'll vomit," he moaned.

"Shh. There now. Shh," I murmured.

How long we remained crouched beside each other on the cold floor I do not know. But as his sobbing gave way to ragged breaths, I noticed a shadow grow longer on the wall next to us, and my heart began to flail like some trapped creature, for fear it was his mother. I dared not look.

"Emily." Maximillian's arms went around us both. "Is he all right?"

"I think so."

Long fingers stroked my cheek. "You're always there."

"I think he came looking for his mother to beg forgiveness."

Maximillian carried his child inside my room, held him close, and set him down on my bed. To my astonishment, the boy was fast asleep.

Max turned to me then, and I felt his presence with every wakened pulse, with every fiber of my being. His gaze ran all over my wispy nightgown, up to my face, and back down to my bare toes which curled against the floorboards. He closed the distance between us, and I melted into his arms, feeling his strong thigh slide between my own, feeling his soft mouth crash down on mine with the urgency of an unleashed storm, feeling the fevered possessiveness of his hands. I abandoned myself to this tempest like some wild blossom on the wind.

When at last he released me, he staggered backward, his blue eyes burning into mine. "Another minute," he admitted hoarsely, "and I'd be lost."

A tear slipped down my cheek. "What are we to do, Max? Do you know?"

He came to me again, caressing me tenderly. "We'll think of something. Once she moves out, it will be easier." His finger lifted my chin. "I love you," he said. "I love you with all my heart."

He held me tightly against him then, and I wept. For the nasty notes, for Demel's treachery, and Iris' threat I clung to him, seeking the comfort I long needed.

"I'm so afraid." I shuddered.

"Not you, too?" he whispered, smiling.

"I'm terrified of her, Max. She warned me. Before I went to bed Iris promised revenge for what happened tonight at the soirée 'right under her nose,' as she put it."

"She should be the last person to use that expression."

"That's what I told her."

He laughed softly. "I wish I'd been there. How did she respond to that?"

"She said I'd pay."

"The bitch."

"That's why I'm scared."

"Don't be. She'll take it out on me, not you."

I shook my head. "I'm not so sure."

Peter's restless stirring caused us to look over at him. I quickly told Max how Iris had slapped him the day before. Max suddenly looked grieved and tired, terribly strained. "Meet me in the clinic tomorrow, and we'll talk."

"I can't go there."

"Why not?"

"I can't explain right now." I pointed to his son.

"I'll work out a way for us to meet," he said, scooping up his son. "Then we'll talk."

"Papa," Peter whimpered. "Put out that candle . . . smells bad." The child was talking gibberish. There was no candle in the room.

Tenderly Maximillian kissed the child's forehead. "I'll fix it," he promised. "Don't worry."

I opened the chamber door and watched them go down the hall. Before climbing back into bed, I plucked a rose from my bouquet and placed it on my pillow. Its sweet scent reminded me of heavenly music, dizzying spins, two giddy hearts, and the joy of our love. I was soon fast asleep.

In morning's light I found it.

From my bed I stared at the envelope I'd missed the night before and felt my eyes grow wide with alarm. *No! Not another!*

But there it was, white and crisp, in front of the door. Too clean, I thought. It couldn't have been there last night. We would have stepped on it—which might mean, my thundering heart realized, someone saw us, then slipped the envelope under the door.

Weak-kneed, I stooped to pick it up. And, as I read the third frightening message, a lump of fear rose in my throat.

The devil's trumpet will call for you with grim and final consequence.

Again, the tiny scrawl. Whose?

Iris'?

Most likely, I thought wildly, stumbling back to my bed. I sat on its edge, crumbling the offensive paper into a ball.

No, a voice inside me counseled. *Save it.*

There was a soft tap at the door. Quickly I reached for my black reticule and stuffed the letter inside. "Come in," I said.

"Oh, miss, you're up." Hannelore sounded surprised. She put her hands to her cheeks. "The boy's been askin' me to let him in to see you for the last hour. I'll tell him you're gettin' dressed."

I looked beyond the maid's shoulder and saw Peter in the hallway. His small hand waved broadly to me, and I wiggled my fingers in reply.

"Do you see what I mean?" she asked me, exasperated. Turning to Peter, she said, "Miss Hopkins is not quite ready. You should wait for her downstairs."

Peter mumbled a protest.

"You'll have to come with me," Hannelore told him before closing my door.

If Peter did go downstairs, he must have climbed right back up, for when I went into the hall, I saw him waiting patiently in the parlor across from my room.

"Guess what, guess what," he shouted, running to greet me.

"I can't imagine," I confessed.

"We're going to the Prater today," he sang.

"Who is?"

"Papa, me, and you."

I smiled in spite of myself. Surely *I* would not be included in an outing to the amusement park while Iris sat by, watching. "And what about your mother?" I asked. "Isn't she going?"

"We spoke to her, and she can't."

"You and your father asked her?" I needed clarification.

He nodded. "And Mama told me to ask you."

"She did?" I was incredulous.

He nodded again, vigorously. "Will you go?"

In truth, I wanted to. I hadn't been to the park since my father had taken me, and I wanted to be with Maximillian and Peter. But why would Iris suggest they bring me? It didn't make sense. I was filled with apprehension at the thought that she was scheming, but how could I disappoint Peter?

He tugged at my hand. "Say yes. Please say yes."

What could I do? I could never hurt the boy. And then I thought Maximillian would be there. *What could go wrong?* I looked down into Peter's tumultuous eyes and replied, "I would love to."

His face brightened instantly. "I'll tell Papa." He scampered off, shirttails flying.

By midafternoon we met in the grand circular driveway. Maximillian boosted Peter up into the carriage, then turned to assist me.

"How did you manage this?" I whispered, placing a hand on his shoulder.

His fingers settled on my waist, and he winked wickedly. "And to think," he whispered, "right under her nose." Then he quickly lifted me up, climbed behind me and sat next to his son.

"How long will it take, Papa?"

Max settled back and laughed. The sound was deep and husky. "A little while," he told the grinning boy.

And so, without a backward glance at the gloomy mansion and with high anticipation for the few precious hours ahead, I relaxed in the velvet cushions, well content. It was pure joy to hear Peter's bright chatter, to see Maximillian turn and look at his son without that bleak, despairing expression so often on his face. We appeared, even to the most casual glance, a happy family on holiday, listening to Papa's commentary on the passing sights, smiling at his jokes, eager to arrive at our destination.

"Are we almost there?"

"Not quite, my impatient pup," Max replied, squeezing the small hand that touched his sleeve.

"I can't wait to see the 'lectrocutions."

"The what!" I exclaimed.

"My tutor told me there's a booth where you can line up to get big shocks."

I turned to Max, dumbfounded.

"It's a fad," he explained. "Young men, show-offs, buy themselves jolts of electricity."

"Sounds foolhardy to me."

"It is. Many are carted off to hospitals because the voltage isn't always safe, though it's supposed to be. Higher voltage," he added dryly, "attracts a bigger crowd."

"Peter," I exclaimed, "this is very dangerous!"

"Well, Mama wants 'lectricity in her new house. Won't that be safe?"

"There, yes," replied Max sternly. "But at an amusement park where people are trying to make money at the expense of others, no." He was emphatic.

"Sorry, Papa. I was only—"

Max didn't let him finish. "It's all right. You didn't know. Stay by us, and everything will be fine."

The carriage wheels no longer clattered on the cobbles and began to slow on a soft earthen track. Nearby, throngs of people milled around pavilions decorated with gaily strung lanterns and colorful banners.

When the carriage door opened, we heard music, singing, all manner of merrymaking. In the next minute we were part of the noisy, jostling crowd.

Wide-eyed, Peter said, "I'd like to try that, Papa." He pointed to a man who had a violin under his chin and a bass drum anchored on his back. Drumsticks with large balled tips were tied to his feet. While he played the fiddle, he kicked back high enough with each footstep to beat the drum.

"That and a horn in your mouth," Max shouted against the rhythmic booms, "and we'll all need rags for our ears."

We were silly, completely caught up in the contagion of the merry Viennese. Waltzes, folk songs, and even serious music came from café bandstands. Those too poor to enter listened from the edge of the pavilion. Children in peasant dress formed circles and danced themselves dizzy while singing familiar rhymes.

Maximillian turned to me. "Everything is an occasion for celebration in Vienna."

"It seems life itself is a fete," I replied.

"What's that, Papa?" Peter pointed abruptly to our left where another group of musicians stood stiff and wooden.

"It's a mechanical orchestra," Maximillian explained. "Each figure represents a different nation." He crouched down to his son. "Look, the Austrian is playing a flute; the Frenchman, a clarinet. The violinist is English and the cellist, American."

"But what are those scary creatures behind the musicians?"

There was a devil behind the Austrian and a grotesque monkey behind the figure of Uncle Sam. I shuddered at the thought of the similar, smaller mechanical piece I'd found one night among the boxes at the sanitarium. "I think the monkey is the conductor, Peter. See, he has a baton in his hand."

The boy looked at me, puzzled. "Then how come he's not standing in front of the musicians?"

"Good question," I replied.

"You ask too many, my little sleuth," said Maximillian. Taking Peter's hand and mine, he led us into a wine garden. "A little refreshment is in order about now, hmm, Emily?"

"May I have a strawberry phosphate, Papa?"

Maximillian looked at me, astonished, then ruffled his son's hair. "You may have anything you want."

As we placed our orders, the air swelled again with song. The tables were filled with women in dirndl skirts, men in lederhosen, or in hunting attire, or in the uniform of their regiments: pink trousers and blue jackets if they were Hussars, silvery green if they came from the Tyrol. They sang drinking songs, carefree songs. Others sounded melancholy.

"Why the sadness?" I remarked to Maximillian.

"Don't you know that the Viennese thrive on sentiment and nostalgia? Popular songs praise their goodness and their magical city, but sometimes they dwell on times gone by and sound regretful."

To our amazement, Peter asked for some of the sausage our buxom waitress placed before us. He appeared to enjoy his drink as much as we savored our wine—new wine, it was. He wanted to get a better look at the wares of a passing hawker, but his father discouraged this.

"Well, can I go see that funny orchestra again? You can watch from here, Papa."

"If you promise to be careful and not wander off."

Maximillian's eyes followed his son as he wove through the crush of people. Satisfied of his safety, Max turned to me. "Did you see him eat?"

"Almost a whole bratwurst." I smiled.

"And I didn't have to prod him."

"That's the point. No one likes to be forced to eat."

Maximillian turned the stem of his wineglass without lifting it from the table. "That's only part of the answer, Emily. It doesn't account for his nightmares."

"They're terrifying," I agreed.

"This isn't exactly dinner table conversation, but the child is afraid of . . . throwing up."

"I know."

"Where does that fear come from? I can't figure it out."

I shook my head. "He does eat, mostly when he thinks no one is looking. I've seen him. Why isn't he afraid of vomiting then?"

Maximillian looked over my head to check on his son. He must have caught Peter's eye, for he smiled, waved energetically, then returned his attention to me. "I haven't a clue," he said with sad finality.

I didn't want to cut Max short. It was important that he talk about his worries, but we had little time together, and I had yet to tell him of my problems with Demel.

"Not to change the subject, Max, but I think I should tell you why I'm practically forbidden to go into the clinic."

"Yes, I'm curious," he replied.

I told him about Demel's blackmail threat, about the press showing up, about the medicine Demel put in the coffee and how it made me sick.

Shocked, Maximillian grabbed the sides of the table and leaned forward. "Why didn't you tell me?"

"It just happened. I've been too frightened to say a word."

"What got into Franz Demel? I can't believe it. Atropine, you say?"

"Or some such substance. Something terrible is going on in that asylum. I'm afraid to go back there. I'm afraid of Iris . . . even here," I admitted. Then I started to describe the notes.

Maximillian's horrified gaze lifted past my shoulder. Next I saw him stand, his face a mask of worry. He moved away from the table. "I don't see Peter," he muttered.

I stood, too. The crowd had thinned, yet there was no sign of the child.

Max looked at me. "We'll talk more about this tonight. I'll come to your room." He left two gulden on the table. "Meantime, let's look for Peter. He's gone off, the rascal."

"Where shall we meet?" I asked.

"At the carriage."

Maximillian lunged toward the other side of the pavilion, cutting through the revelers with ease. I went in the opposite direction, back to the mechanical orchestra where Peter was told to stay. The grotesque faces of the devil and monkey made others laugh, but they seemed to mock me. I turned from them quickly and followed a less frequented path which I thought circled the exhibit.

A hiker carrying a walking stick with ribbons and flowers tied to it greeted me. "*Grüss Gott,*" he said.

"*Grüss Gott,*" I said and smiled.

A family sat on a bench under a huge beech tree. While the mother knitted and the father dozed, a child played with a dog. There were other children nearby, many of them, but no Peter. I hurried on.

What seemed like an interminable time later I came upon a magnificent secluded area with lamps, an open-air stage bordered by lovely gazebos. Recognizing it as the garden of the Hotel Sacher, the gathering place of Austria's aristocracy, I paused for a moment.

"May I help you, miss?"

I explained to the waiter that I was looking for the way back to my carriage, for surely Maximillian had found Peter and awaited me there. I described where we had entered the park, and to my relief the young man knew the exact entrance.

"If you follow the track around the Prater, you'll have no trouble."

"I get lost easily," I confessed.

"See that path?" My eyes followed the direction of his pointing finger. "Start there. When the path forks, you can only go one of two ways. Go left. It won't be hard."

Reassured, I started off. I took but a few steps and found myself at a chaotic convergence of paths. *Left here? So soon? Wouldn't he have said as much? He must mean farther on.*

I continued walking, never finding the clear division the waiter described. I thought of retracing my steps, but the path behind me was narrow while the way ahead was wider and less isolated from the rest of the park. At the next turn, a man wearing a red bandanna and gold earring started to strum his guitar. He spoke to me when I passed him, and I felt my heart jump to my throat.

The afternoon was wearing on, and the crowd was rapidly thinning. There was no sign of Maximillian, Peter, or anything familiar.

Then I did recognize something—a fence, exactly like the one where the coachman had left the carriage. I would come to it if I followed this fence. I turned again and stared up ahead. Beyond the knots of people I saw two lone figures, one large, one small. They were hand in hand. I started to run. "Max, Peter," I called.

Men and women were laughing and swaying together. They stared at me. More bandannas and swarthy faces. A lewd remark. I cringed and moved forward, following the fence.

A hawker shrieked. I had to look away from him and hold my breath, for the smell of his greasy bratwurst and stale beer turned my stomach. On I went, my eye to that fence. It wound through a grouping of fir trees. Did someone slip back into their shadows?

I hurried on, not liking the growing darkness, the chill in the breeze, or the way it hissed through the pine boughs. But here was my fence. This was the way.

Someone was watching me. I could sense it.

Then, an instant later, the pole lamps went on. I could see these lights through the branches. Everything wasn't against me. I began to smile.

Just as a heavy hand fell on my shoulder.

My mouth was dry as dust. I twisted away and lunged forward, away from that beefy grasp.

There was a vulgar curse, a loud belch. "You'll not escape me again."

I heard a coarse laugh and the shatter of glass. They startled me long enough to be caught.

"I like me a bitch with fire," spewed a harsh voice, terrifyingly familiar.

I saw the bloated face, recognized the sour breath, and cringed under his savage scowl. He was one of the two who had attacked me in the rose garden the night I arrived.

"Thought you'd get away a second time, did ya?" He smirked, burping once more. "We was told you'd be here and came to collect." He nodded drunkenly.

"Who told you?" I asked, trying to jerk my arm free.

His mouth spread in a slack grin. "Frau Schaller. Now *there's* a piece." He snickered wildly.

Despite my terror, two facts struck me at once. Iris had cunningly arranged this nastiness, and the man was horribly drunk.

His fingers bit into my arm. "Ya got us fired, ya know." Another ugly belch. He wobbled backward, dragging me with him. He stumbled, and I bent my mouth to his wrist, biting down hard.

He let go, cursing furiously. I sprang forward into the light. I ran as fast as I could away from his demented laugh.

Daylight had faded eerily. All was silent now, save for the gritty noise of my shoes on the dirt, a harsh sound to my raw nerves. I couldn't wait until I was safe in the carriage and heading back to the mansion.

I thought I heard a neigh. Gasping for breath, I rounded a corner, and there were the carriages lining the street like strands of big black pearls. With delirious relief I moved in between them, careful to avoid the restive stamp of the horses.

Where was the huge gilded *D*—the undeniable symbol of Dr. Demel's narcissism? Where were Maximillian and Peter? A shiver of fear rippled through me anew. Then I noticed a brougham standing by itself, diagonally across the street.

"Please, dear Lord, let it be," I whispered aloud, making my way to it.

There was the *D*, a golden beacon in the night. And there was the coachman, jumping down to assist me. I sank into the velvet cushions, exhausted, facing the rear of the carriage. I was about to ask the driver if he'd seen Max and Peter when I swore I saw them running toward me. I knelt on the oppo-site seat, my face at the window, knowing the rear carriage lights would expose my presence. I waved. They waved back, smiling, running faster.

To my puzzlement, I watched Max's gaze lift above me. His expression became shocked, anguished. At the same moment, I sensed the shift of some weight on the roof, heard the crack of a whip, and felt the jolt of the carriage as it sprang forward.

"Halt! *Halt!*" Max shouted.

Frozen with terror, I watched the carriage door slowly open.

✝ Chapter Twelve

A dark figure swung inside. "There were two of us, remember?"

I pressed myself into the farthest corner of the seat. I'd never forgotten this man, his friend, or the coachman, for that matter. In fact, he appeared to be a collaborator, driving off at just the right moment.

"Now I'll have you all to myself."

"Don't you dare touch me!"

His smirk caused the scar above his mouth to lengthen in a deadly line. I watched his hand come closer, felt rough fingers scrape my cheek and move to the clasp of my cloak.

"No!" I cried, pushing at his hand. But his smile grew wider, showing black gaps between his pointed teeth which were set in a small mouth amidst sharp features. He was a little weasel of a man.

"You owe me." He snickered, moving a filthy finger across my chin.

I shrank away. "The driver will stop," I cried.

Again, the cruel half-laugh and half-sneer. "He won't, m'dear. He's afraid I'll squeal on him. He guessed faster than anyone what's goin' on in that place, and he made the mistake of tellin' me."

"What place?" I would say anything to stall him and protect myself.

"The asylum. It's only a matter of time before the dirty

secret's out and the bitch gets her due. High and mighty, she is."

"Who? Frau Schaller?"

With his free hand, he reached into his pocket, pulled out a wad of money, and fingered it greedily. "Generous, ain't she?"

"You're blackmailing her."

The beady eyes tightened. "Like I say, only a matter of time . . . like in this coach." He leaned closer. "So, you goin' to give it to me handy, or make it harder for us both?"

"Scum! That's what you are," I cried.

The motion of the jolting coach gave me some advantage. He reached for me and missed. With a coarse laugh he lunged again, this time ripping open my cloak and tearing the collar from my dress. "This ain't my way. I gave ya a choice."

"Don't sicken me."

That was all he needed. He flung himself on me, and I thrashed back, my arms and legs flailing against his clawing hands. In terror, I watched one brutal fist draw back, and just when it would have landed on my face, the brougham veered sharply to the right, causing my assailant to lose his balance.

He cursed savagely from the floor, and to his shock and mine, the carriage kept turning. We were going back. I heard the coachman's cry as he set the horses to a frantic pace.

Furious and surprised, the little weasel turned to me with murderous eyes. He held a knife.

I screamed.

"Quiet, or I'll use it." He smiled, satisfied anew.

The knife was dangerously close to my throat in the speeding carriage, and when it bounced in a rut, I could not help myself. I screamed again and again, blood-chilling screams.

The carriage slowed to a stop.

Then, from somewhere beside it, I heard shouts and curses. The door flung open. I could see another conveyance.

My attacker's smile altered dramatically. He was thrown to the ground near the second carriage, and he was pummeled by the coachman . . . and Max.

† † †

Peter slept through the commotion. He stirred briefly in his father's arms when he was transferred to my carriage. The coachman held open its door.

"I tried to shake him off the roof by starting off fast," he explained.

Was this an apology? I stared at the man.

"I tried to warn ya from the beginning," he said, closing the door.

I sank into the cushions, on the same side as Maximillian. We held hands across the sleeping Peter's lap.

"We'll talk at length when we're home," he told me, looking down at his son. "He may wake up."

I squeezed Max's hand.

For a while I said nothing, but I was so troubled by my thoughts that I could not keep them to myself for long.

"She kept her word, Max."

"Who?"

I glanced at Peter for a quick second, looked up and mouthed the name I-ris. "She paid the two toughs who attacked me my first night at the asylum—the ones you fired—to track me down at the Prater." I shivered. "One got to me before I found the carriage. The other waited for me near it."

A muscle in Maximillian's jaw twitched. "I could kill her for it!"

"She's also paying one of the men to keep quiet about the deaths in the clinic," I added.

"What would *he* know about them?"

"I'm not sure, but he implied Iris knew quite a bit, and he showed me a roll of bills he said she paid him."

Maximillian's face grew dark and shuttered. For long moments he looked at his son; his expression tense, his eyes full of pain. "When I think of what this child has to endure because of his mother, I could weep," he said with raw desperation.

"Where was Peter? Where did you find him? I looked all over and got lost. The rest you know."

"He was on the other side of our pavilion, looking for us."

"Why did he leave his spot in front of that god-awful orchestra?"

"Somebody became ill there and vomited. Peter's so terrified of it, he ran back to us. I couldn't see him in the crowd."

"He suffers terribly, doesn't he?"

Max's voice was soft and sad. "Yes."

When we approached the mansion's gates, the carriage did not go straight through them. It paused halfway so that the gaudy, gilded, monstrous *D* was at eye level, staring back at me like some shameless mask of deceit. Why did the coachman hesitate? Had some small nocturnal animal crossed before the conveyance? Was the man himself reluctant to go forward, or was he warning me once again? I felt the sterile silence, the soulless quality of this place as I had the first time I passed through these gates, only now I feared that the malevolent forces at work here would twist out of control.

I couldn't relax that night. I kept thinking about my fright at the Prater, about what my assailants told me. I became more terrified of Iris. The woman had not a shred of conscience. It seemed like forever before Maximillian came to my door.

"Quick, come in."

"Sorry, it took a while to settle Peter."

"I'm not surprised."

Max took my hands in his. "How are you? I'm worried about you, too."

"We've all been through a lot," I said shakily. "But I'm calming down. Now that you're here, I feel better."

"Good." He smiled and drew me into his embrace.

Voices from the hall drifted through the door. Excited, urgent voices. Rapid speech, followed by anxious, repeated knocking—right on my door.

Demel burst in, with Hannelore behind him. His eyes were aflame at the sight of Maximillian and me. I heard his sharp intake of breath, witnessed that sickening, knowing smirk of his, saw his patting hands smooth back the waves of his hair.

"So here you are, Maximillian." Demel's voice was cool.

I staggered out of Max's arms.

"Yes." Maximillian's reply was noncommittal.

"Best you come with me," Demel said.

"Where, at this late hour?"

"The clinic. There's an emergency."

My heart went berserk, beating with the frenzy of a snare drum. I looked to the stricken Hannelore for some measure of the problem. But she could only return my stare numbly while she nervously wiped her palms on her apron.

"What's happened?" I whispered into the tense silence. "Another patient? No," I cried, "it can't be."

"It isn't," replied Demel tightly. His eyes were knowing, mocking, provocative. They were fixed on Maximillian.

My terrified gaze went back and forth between the two. I was breathless, fearing the worst, yet totally unprepared for Demel's statement.

"It's your wife, Max. She's dead!"

"Dead?" came Maximillian's shocked whisper.

"Murdered. You'd better come."

When they left, I turned to Hannelore. "How did Dr. Demel know Maximillian was here?"

She looked down. "Sorry, miss. There was no answer at Dr. Schaller's door, or Peter's . . . and Dr. Demel kept sayin' real angry: 'Where is the man? Where is he?' "

"Is Peter still asleep?"

"I think so. Don't be mad at me," she pleaded. "I couldn't help it. I'm scared."

"It's all right, Hannelore. We're all upset."

I wanted to go to the clinic, but dared not while Demel was there. Tomorrow I would, though. I would find an excuse to go there.

†   †   †

When morning came, I decided to find Peter first. I didn't have to look far. He and his father were in the parlor across from my room. There were tears in Peter's eyes and dark shadows around Maximillian's. My heart went out to both.

"Oh, Peter," I said. "I'm so sorry."

The little boy ran to me, crying pitifully.

"He wanted to come here," Max explained. "He needs your comfort."

"I give it gladly," I said, hugging Peter tightly.

"Everything is changed," he wailed.

I nodded and gave him a kiss.

"I don't want things to be different. I want them to be the way they used to be. Just Mama, Papa, and me. And no Ringstrasse house."

"I know," I agreed.

"Just the three of us . . . all together," he went on.

"I understand."

He drew away, his blue eyes solemn. "No, you don't. You can't."

"I think I can," I replied. "You see, my mother died when I was a little girl."

Peter took several moments to absorb this. When he spoke, his eyes searched mine. "How did she die?"

"In childbirth . . . the baby, too." I saw a round tear glistening in his eyelashes and felt my own eyes grow moist. "But I still had my father. So do you."

He appeared to weigh this information. Then he admitted, "I was angry at Mama for wanting to move away. Then she got angry with me."

"No—"

"Yes," he corrected sharply. "She said I was skinny . . . she didn't love me anymore."

It was a shame his last memories of his mother were painful. I had to address them. "She did love you, Peter. She always brought you nice surprises when she returned from trips. She wanted you to have fun. Didn't she suggest you go to the Prater?"

"Yes, but . . ."

"She showed her feelings to you in a different way than your father does. But she loved you nonetheless."

"I hope so." He sniffled, reaching for his father's hand.

Max pulled him close. "Sometimes terrible things happen, and nobody can explain them. Over time you learn to accept them, and I'll help you accept what happened to Mama."

"You won't let anything happen to you, Papa, will you?"

Max looked at me. "Not if I can help it."

"Promise?"

With all his soul in his eyes, he turned to his son. "I give you my word."

While Max dried Peter's eyes, I walked to an armchair and picked up one of several books, *The Story of Hero*.

"Did you bring this for me, Peter?"

He ran to me. "I hoped you could read it."

"Well," intoned Max, "while you two become engrossed in *Hero,* I'll return to the clinic. God knows I'm needed there." He took a deep breath and brushed by me, whispering, "Thank you for all your help."

I smiled in return and sat down with Peter. "Now where did we leave off?"

"I told you the whole story. Don't you remember?"

"And you want to read it again?"

"It's my favorite. I read it almost every day."

I wondered why. What was it about the story that captivated the child? Why did it speak to him so meaningfully?

I found out when we got to Hero's dilemma. The dog could not decide whether to tell the other toy animals he knew something that they didn't—something they really should be aware of.

At this point in the story, Peter suddenly said, "I don't like to throw up, Miss Hopkins."

I had no idea why he would mention this now. But since his eating habits and health were a concern to most people in the house, I encouraged him to speak about them.

"Somebody vomited at the Prater yesterday. That's why I left to find you."

"What's so terrible about getting sick? Once it's over, you feel much better."

Eyes as big as saucers, he stared at me as if I had two heads. "How do you know that?"

"I've experienced it."

"You have?"

"Most people have."

Peter's eyebrows came together. He studied me shrewdly, and then he suddenly looked incredibly sad and disbelieving. "My mama vomited. Then she died."

I had heard Iris was poisoned. I was surprised to learn that Peter knew it and other nasty details of his mother's death.

"That was different. She drank something that caused her to . . ." I didn't finish my thought. I didn't have to. The fear in Peter's eyes was as strong as the terror of his dreams. We finished Hero's story, praising the dog for telling his friends to hide so they wouldn't be rounded up and shipped off to homes of the needy which wouldn't be as nice as the one they lived in.

Then Peter surprised me again. "But if Hero didn't warn the others, wouldn't poor children have more toys, Miss Hopkins?"

I was touched by the child's sensitivity. "You're such a good person," I said. I was impressed by him and by the burden of responsibility he felt, for it was becoming clear to me that he was putting together, perhaps erroneously, bits and pieces of things that he'd heard or witnessed in this awful asylum. Whatever they were, the facts were too terrifying for him to think or talk about. That's why they surfaced in nightmares. I wanted to ask him more questions, but decided against probing and pressing the child after all he had been through this morning.

"That's quite a story," I said, closing the book.

Peter agreed, asked me the time, and announced regretfully that his tutor was coming.

"We'll continue tomorrow," I replied.

He left, I thought, feeling somewhat relieved, while I felt increasingly troubled. I crossed to my room, donned my cloak and bonnet, then went through the long corridors and out to the garden. I needed fresh air.

Peter knew something. Even if he was not consciously aware of it, he knew something that he was afraid to tell us. He was afraid to eat, fearful of vomiting. During his nightmare, he had rambled on about this, and about candles and smoke. There was no question in my mind that his fears were related to the mysterious deaths in the clinic. I wanted to help the child with his problems. I loved him as much as I loved his father.

Now there would be no more secret meetings for Maximillian and me, no more stolen pleasures. Our love could be openly and freely expressed. But for how long?

If his wife was murdered, surely he and I would be suspect. Dr. Demel saw the two of us the previous night. Werner knew about us, as did Hannelore and the other servants.

What irony! I thought. I came to Vienna to clear my father's name, and I would end up having to clear my own and Maximillian's. Who would have dreamed that just over a year ago I, the woman destined to join her father in the hallowed world of medicine, would be burdened with the guilt of his death, would seek to vindicate him and in so doing have to vindicate herself and her lover? The more life changes, the more it stays the same, I marveled.

But back home in Philadelphia I was afraid to take action. I let those who intimidated me win out. I wouldn't now. I couldn't. My love for Maximillian and Peter gave me the courage that I heretofore had not known I possessed.

There was only Dr. Demel to contend with. Iris was dead.

I was pacing back and forth, I realized, like some creature in its cage. Willfully, almost greedily, I decided to take charge of the events in my life, rather than respond passively to them. Demel had frightened and taunted me like some cat with a mouse. My restive steps became purposeful strides, and they led me to the back of his mansion. If my guess was right, the small room without windows, the alcove that held the coffin the night I arrived, was in this section of the house. I went back inside and up several steps, through a narrow passage, around a dark corner, and found this queer little room.

It was completely empty—as it was when I first sought refuge here—except for the draperies. Dark as midnight, weighted by mystery and shadows, they beckoned to me. Parting their dusty folds, I slipped behind them. There was only a wall, hard to the touch and windowless. Nothing more.

I turned, about to leave, not really knowing why I was here, and felt my foot brush some protrusion in the flooring. On hands and knees, I groped for this curious knot of wood which had proved, so far, to be the single irregularity in this room of wearisome sameness.

There was a groan, the ache of timber against timber. I pulled harder at the protuberance and, to my shock, the floor-boards lifted ever so slightly. With all my might, I yanked at them and stared down into a gaping black hole. *Were there steps?*

Yes! With shaking fingers, I felt hollow risers. The laddered steps plunged downward. Hiding my cloak and hat behind the draperies, I sucked in my breath and forced myself toward what appeared to be a pit.

The rungs were sturdy, not old. I had discovered, no doubt, some little-known way to the cellars, and I wondered if they could be reached from the outside.

There was a drop from the last rung to the floor. I could see it because of the dim light coming around an ell up ahead. Holding my skirts, I made the small jump and landed upright, to my relief. Surely no female used this hidden stair-way.

It required considerable self-prodding to go forward, but I followed that light. I rubbed my arms against the dampness. My nose wrinkled at the smell of mold and something else I could not name, but I was curious about the source of that light.

I proceeded carefully to a partition of sorts, beyond which I dared not go. For, when I put my eye to a crack in its wood, I saw that I had reached a crypt, a large niche carved into the mansion's foundation. And to my quaking horror, I thought I had come upon the devil himself.

✝ Chapter Thirteen

All I could see through the crack was a caped figure with its back to me hovering over a table, peering into . . . I know not what. Flames shot up and outwards from this demon's frenzied efforts. Turned half toward me, the face, though veiled in curls of steam, lit with a crazed look of joy. With the same ghastly rapture, an arm waved triumphantly in the air while boots tattooed a *danse macabre* on the stones. I turned and fled, hearing a flat, disjointed melody, an incantation that I could ascribe to neither a male nor female voice. It was a demented sound, a wail that could only come from a deranged person.

A patient?

Up the ladder I flew. Retrieving my cloak and hat, I fled down corridors and upstairs to my room and closed the door. I sagged against it, breathless and frightened by what I had seen.

But what had I seen? The answer, I felt, lay in the clinic.

I changed swiftly into my navy day dress, trimmed with raspberry buttons and braidings. I undid my hair and was brushing it when Hannelore knocked and told me she wanted to speak to me.

"Yes?" I said expectantly.

"I saw you running and wanted to know if anythin' was wrong."

"No, nothing, thank you." She was about to leave when I stopped her. "But I would like some help with my hair."

A ripple of relief spread across her honest face. She picked up the brush but did not immediately use it. Instead she began to chat. I wondered if I should have asked for her help. She was fingering and handling my hair as if there was all the time in the world, when I needed to go to the clinic! Then she began talking about Iris, and I decided she could dawdle as long as she wanted.

"Shockin' it was, the way they found her body."

"Where was that?"

"In the clinic."

"I thought she was brought there to be revived."

"Nay, miss. She was already there, in Johann's room. The two of them were lovers, it turned out."

"She got sick while she was with him?"

Hannelore nodded. "From the wine she drank."

"And Johann stayed well?"

"As far as I know, he did."

I wondered if the wine was like the coffee given me, only stronger. And I wondered who had poisoned it. Demel? In a fit of jealousy, Johann? I was becoming increasingly curious about the clinic. Hannelore's next words were like music to my ears.

"Course, it's been awful hard for Professor Doctor Demel. Poor man was up half the night. So I was glad when he told me he was settling down for a rest and I should keep everyone from his door."

"When did you talk to him?"

"Just now."

I grinned. "Hannelore, you can leave my hair down. A ribbon is all it needs."

KLINIK, the sign above me read. I paused to draw a fortifying breath, then knocked, pushed down the handle, and to my astonishment the door opened.

Bertha glanced up, and her face tightened as though she fought surprise. "It's very busy here, Miss Hopkins. We have two new admissions, and they've come at a bad time."

"Then perhaps you might want an extra pair of hands."

A vein pulsed at her temple. "We don't."

I disregarded her rudeness and walked to Frau Steinmetz's room. The door was open, the room empty. I was surprised and must have shown it, for another patient came over to me.

"She's not here," he said.

"Has she gone for a walk?"

The man shrugged his shoulders and shuffled off, his face and posture reflecting the morbid gloom that filled the room. Iris' death was the third such incident to occur in this sanitarium since my arrival. No wonder the atmosphere was tense. Everybody was affected, especially Johann, her lover, in whose room she died.

The gardener was near the solarium where I had first seen him working with Friedericke. He sat, despondent, eyes focused on his hands which were folded in his lap. The instant he saw me, he straightened and studied me with a cold, piercing intensity. Then, still staring, he got up to leave. That was when I noticed fear beneath the cold contempt in his eyes.

Why this affected me as deeply as it did, I could scarcely explain to myself. My thoughts went to Iris, and I wondered what lie she might have told Johann. What rumor might she have started? She knew what lay behind the deaths here, according to the men who attacked me. Was she responsible for them? Did she act alone? It was possible she had even tried to implicate me in this unspeakable evil. And what of the creature in the cellars? How did that one figure into the grizzly picture?

I turned suddenly, and to my shock and profound sadness, I realized I might be staring at a clue!

Frau Steinmetz. In she came, through the unlocked door. My eyes were riveted on her navy cloak, her disheveled hair, her flushed face. Without speaking to me, she walked to her room, returning moments later with her embroidery.

"You've made considerable progress, Frau Steinmetz." I offered the compliment to encourage conversation, but she was of no mind to respond. In truth, her needlework had deteriorated. There were more of those strange horn-shaped flowers on the cloth, but they ran across each other haphazardly rather than follow a thought-out, neatly stitched pattern. The cotton itself was dirty, and with each stab of the needle, Frau Steinmetz grunted.

It was a grim decoration, but not as ghoulish as the thing another patient put before me now.

"Do you like it?" she asked in a quaking voice.

I clapped a hand to my mouth. "Where did you find such a thing?"

"It was given to me," she responded, indignant. When she moved a tiny lever, two miniature monkeys under the glass bell waltzed, just as they did in the mechanical piece in storage. Just as they did in the large orchestra in the Prater.

"It's a death waltz," she said gruesomely. "Like here."

On those words, Frau Steinmetz whined. Furiously she began to stitch another floppy black flower.

"There, there, now, Frau Steinmetz." It was Maximillian's voice. He gave her a warm, approving pat on the shoulder. "No need to get upset." He turned to me. "I'd like to speak with you, Miss Hopkins."

I followed him to his office. "Max, the patients are suffering terribly. The atmosphere here is not good for their health."

"Franz Demel just admitted two new patients."

"They could not have come at a worse time."

"I know," Max agreed.

"Why did he do it?"

"Maybe he felt he had to so things would look normal. He's afraid of bad publicity. Maybe he didn't want to turn away business."

"It must be exhausting for you," I said sympathetically. "Are they elderly?"

"Why do you ask that?"

"I was thinking of Herr Kirsch. His illness and his age hid the fact that he was poisoned. I'm sure of it. I wouldn't want anyone else to suffer the same fate."

"One is almost as old as Herr Kirsch, the other isn't. Neither has Herr Kirsch's problems."

My medical training took over just then. "What's wrong with them?"

"They're physically and mentally exhausted. Headaches, insomnia. They're anxious and irritable."

"Classic neurasthenia cases."

"The plague of our times. With so much emphasis on material goods, it's not surprising," Max added dryly.

"I hope they don't become sicker here. Frau Steinmetz has."

"I've noticed."

"She looks unkempt, bizarre. She wasn't in the clinic when I first arrived. Where—"

"I left orders for the doors to stay locked," Max cut in, visibly upset.

"I'd offer to help, but Dr. Demel and Bertha don't want me here."

Maximillian drove a hand through his hair. "It's probably best you stay away."

Something in his tone gave me pause. I searched his face. "What is it? What aren't you telling me?"

He took me in his arms. "Emily," he said quietly, "Johann claims you wanted Iris dead. I think he's told Frau Steinmetz, possibly the others."

My body stiffened with anger and shock. I could feel my scalp tighten. "So that's why she wouldn't speak to me. Neither would he." It took every ounce of will not to get hysterical. "Iris probably bit this out with her last breath. And now Demel will use it. I'll be his scapegoat, Max. Do you know what this means?"

"Yes," he replied wearily. "But don't forget there were deaths here before you came."

I nodded, clinging to him. He held me tight, then stepped back. His eyes were full of hope and trust. "The longer I live, dear Emily, the more I'm convinced that there's a remedy to every difficulty in life. Every puzzle has its own solution. For years I wondered how I would continued to live with Iris. I worried about Peter. Then you came along."

"But I might not be here for long. . . ."

A hint of a smile touched Max's face. "Of course you will. Having found you, do you think I'd let anyone take you away?"

"I wish I had your confidence."

"You will." His voice stayed low. "Maybe Iris' death is unrelated to the others."

"What makes you say that?"

"I can't explain now. I have to get back to the ward, but we'll talk later." He gave me a little kiss. "Now try to relax," he said, and he opened the door.

I left, thinking I should collect myself before anyone noticed my distraught condition. *What better place than the solarium!* Without a word to anyone, I went to it, and was relieved to find myself alone with the flowers.

A richly textured tapestry of shape and color spread before me, a floral display all the more unique, given the time of year. With the sunlight warm on my face, I meandered through fiery paths of burnt-orange and ruby chrysanthemums to a delicate cascade of water. A sweep of lush, exotic plants climbed the wall to the side of this fountain, and I thought as I inhaled their fragrance that I had entered Eden. Oh, the wonder of these flowers. The magic of their gardener, Friedericke!

I sat on a small white bench and allowed my senses to be sweetly seduced. But the fragrance had a mysterious element in it, I thought. Intrigued, I looked more carefully about me, past the orchids and gardenias and rhododendrons, over to a low border of plants that vaguely resembled dwarf hibiscus. Odd little hybrids. And only a few of them. Purple. White. Forced blooms, perhaps.

As I walked toward them, the scent became stronger, somewhat unpleasant. I bent to touch the funnel-shaped blossom, to read the label protruding from the soil. My hair fell forward, and I quickly brushed it from my eyes and face. Datura stramonium. The Latin words meant nothing to me, yet I continued to stare at the marker. To my surprise, I realized that the plants must have come from America, for in parentheses was the word *jimsonweed.* I mouthed the syllables, working them slowly around my tongue. I mumbled aloud. "Jim, Jim, Jimson." The American name touched some dim memory within me, stirred strangely in my head. I moved away, my steps as unsure as my thought. *Jim . . . Jame . . . James.* My mind reached for something it could not quite grasp.

And then, from the nearby potting room there came a piteous wail, a melancholic weeping of such depth that I was compelled toward it. There was a mere instant of quiet. Then the hysterical sobbing came again.

Drooping like a withered blossom, Friedericke was hunched over a worktable. Her shoulders heaved. One chubby hand clutched her breast, and the other trembled at her brow. Aware of my presence, she turned her tear-streaked face to me. So raw and genuine was her pain, it epitomized grief and desolation.

"S-she's dead," the woman cried. "S-she was like a d-daughter to me, and n-now she's g-gone."

"I am sorry, so terribly sorry for your loss."

"And the b-boy has no m-mother. What'll w-we do without h-her?" She wailed again, a pitiful sound, and her fist beat harshly at her chest.

I put my hand on her shoulder, but there was nothing for it. The woman was inconsolable. I could not pretend to mourn Iris. If I did, my insincerity would show, juxtaposed as it would be to Friedericke's honest suffering.

I then thought of Peter and felt a stab of guilt that my selfish wish for his mother's demise had come true. Feeling greatly unsettled, I decided to try once more.

"If there is something I can do . . ." I offered.

Through choked sobs, Friedericke spoke. "Sooo n-nice of y-you."

"Think of something you'd like me to do for you. I love flowers. Perhaps I could help you with them."

The heavy woman took a quivering breath. "M-maybe," she gasped, "we could g-go for a little walk. Get out for a w-while."

"This afternoon?"

She nodded.

"In about an hour?"

She nodded again.

I left, wishing she had wanted me to work in the solarium, because I could easily monitor events in the clinic from there. I also did not wish to be alone with Friedericke for any length of time. What would I say to her if I could not feign sorrow?

On my way out of the potting room, I noticed that several of its glass panes were blackened on one side, giving the glass the properties of a mirror. As I passed the darkened panels, I paused momentarily, wondering at the brightness of my left eye. But I was so involved with my shifting feelings, I thought no more about this, and went on my way.

The house proper was a hive in mourning. Plans for Iris' burial were being made on a scale that mystified me. It seemed as though Dr. Demel and Werner were orchestrating a public pageant, not a family funeral. I could not discern how much the extravagance typified the deceased woman and her need for theatrics, or the society she reflected.

"No, Onkel Franz," Werner was saying, "we should have Lipizzaners, not ordinary horses. The darkest available."

"But silver gray would strike a contrast to the black livery and hearse. Iris would like that."

"It will look smarter if the animals flaunted silver plumes with red roses entwined in their manes."

"To match the floral blanket on the casket," Demel said. "I see your point."

They were discussing the width of the bows on the wreaths and bouquets, and other small details that I regarded as minutiae. But, then, it was not my loved one who died; it was my enemy. Their immortalization of her was disquieting because it made me feel quite apart from them. Isolated. Vulnerable.

My foot had just touched the first wide marble step when I sensed something gliding behind me. I clutched the balustrade and turned.

"Did you know the funeral is the day after tomorrow?" Werner asked.

"I didn't. Thank you."

"You'll ride in the carriage with me. It's already settled." A trace of resentment came into his voice.

"I see."

He shoved his hands into his pockets and stared. "Do you?" I didn't know whether he spoke from sorrow or suppressed anger. Then he added, almost blandly, "Lucky you. Got the man you wanted." Other than a slight shifting in his eyes, his face was unreadable. "My sister is dead."

Not pausing to think of how he would interpret my action, I spun around to climb the stairs.

Once in my room, I sat at my dressing table, hands under my chin, elbows hard on the glass.

Every puzzle holds its own solution, Max had said.

But the problem facing me was an intricate mosaic of deception and lies.

And what was wrong with my eye? It wasn't itchy. It wasn't red. Just bright—sparkling, one would say. My pupil was dilated.

Jim . . . James . . . Jimson . . . The names hovered over me like uncertain whispers, yet I could still attach no meaning to them.

I reached for the little velvet box that held my good luck charm, the medal my father and I had dug up. I clutched it in a tight fist, hoping, I supposed, for some enlightenment, but the frustration I suffered over the word *jimsonweed* did not abate. Getting to my feet, I sighed and changed into a warmer dress, collecting my gloves, cloak, and reticule. Though I was too early to meet Friedericke, I went out the front door anyway.

"Going for a walk, Miss Hopkins?" Dr. Demel asked. "Allow me to join you."

It was the first time I was alone with the man since that dreadful night in his study. I struggled to keep my voice calm. "I'd rather you didn't," I said, and moved on.

"Truly, Miss Hopkins." His laugh was small, fluttery. He caught up with me. "You're in no position to refuse any scrap of help thrown your way."

I stood perfectly still. "From you, Dr. Demel?"

"Yes." Long fingers steepled at his mouth, touched his lips thoughtfully. "You see, we need each other now."

"I can't imagine why."

His smile turned sour, deprecating. "There will be an investigation. Apparently, Iris told Johann with her dying breath that you poisoned her wine." He paused for effect, then spoke with an undercurrent of triumph. "We all know why, don't we?"

"I didn't do it."

"Of course not." He laughed again.

I gripped the side of a trellis. I felt weak, dizzy. What I feared most was becoming real. He was looking at me steadily, studying me, ready to pounce.

"What do you want?"

"To strike a bargain."

"How?"

Demel's tufted brows twitched. "If you say nothing about my blend of coffee, I'll pass off Johann's story as the fabrication of a demented mind."

"It won't be the first time you've used that excuse, will it, Dr. Demel?"

His dark eyes were as smooth as cold marble. "You accept, of course."

I gave a harsh, mocking laugh. "Are you afraid you'll be accused of homicide?"

A pulsing silence fell between us.

"Don't you dare go against me or oppose what I'm doing in my sanitarium. I have enough worries."

"What are you doing?"

"Trying to build a reputable hospital."

"It doesn't look like one anymore. And I won't help you restore it. I trusted you once, Dr. Demel. I placed my father's reputation in your hands, and you blackmailed me." I watched his expression twist into a frightened, caustic leer. I thought the intimidating gesture was born of fear and fueled by degradation. The man was afraid of me, afraid of the fact that I could make *him* look like the murderer. I could claim he made an attempt on my life. Maybe he was the killer—though why he would want to do away with the very patients he needed for a successful business, and why he would want to harm his niece mystified me. But maybe her death was unrelated to the others, as Maximillian suggested. Finally, I told my anxious heart, many people saw me at the Prater the night Iris was poisoned.

Dr. Demel had deceived me. He had used me as I had been used once before by my superiors, but I would not bend to the wicked schemes of any criminal again. Despite the clutching sensation in my chest, I spoke coolly. "No, it's a devil's bargain you offer. I don't accept."

"Time will change that." He chuckled maliciously. "Time will tell."

The echo of that wicked laugh followed me to the back of the mansion where I decided to wait for Friedericke. Demel's warning threaded through my mind, haunting me, as did the half-rotted door upon which my eyes were now fastened. On silent feet I approached it, drawing my cloak closer about me.

Some dark, screeching bird swept before me, and a chilling wind moaned through the feathery pines. "Devil's song," Frau Steinmetz had called it.

The answer is within the problem.

"Where are you going, Miss Hopkins?" came Peter's anxious call. His eyes lowered to the aged wooden door, and his lips quivered.

I paused, wondering at the child's reaction.

"Don't go there," he mumbled, a disturbed, distorted cry.

"Why, Peter?" What did the child know?

He made a valiant effort at control. "It's dirty."

I knew that was not the real reason, and I did not want to upset him further. "I'll take your word for it," I replied, turning around. "I'm going for a walk. Tell Papa to meet me if he can."

The child seemed satisfied.

Once he was gone, I opened the door, more curious than ever, more wary of danger.

To my surprise, the hinges on the timber were well oiled, and a lantern hung from the door's inside handle—facts that bespoke deliberate and frequent use!

Blinking in the darkness, I took my trembling lip between my teeth. I propped the door open with my foot, and reached for one of the phosphorous matches bunched and wedged into fat cracks in the wall.

The lantern's wick soon flared to life. With that signal, I began an uneven, sloping descent, keenly aware that each shaking footfall brought forth squeals and squeaks from shadowed corners I dared not flash the light upon.

Approaching the large stone slabs of the crypt, I paused to focus on the smell. Strong. Acrid. From stale tobacco. From Werner's cigar?

More pungent yet, the odor grew with each laggard step of mine.

I came upon the grotto where last I saw the cloaked fiend. The cavern was deserted now and in ruins.

I could see shattered flasks and tubes, a smashed rusted stand, broken candles. Baffled, I thought of Frau Steinmetz. Her dishevelment. Her morbid stitches. Black flowers—trumpets, she called them.

The horn, the horn 'tis not a thing to laugh or scorn!

My blood took up a frantic coursing. My gaze bent to the bits and pieces of some strange and loathsome alchemy. My hair fell forward over my face, and I quickly brushed it away from my eye, my sparkling eye.

Jim . . . James . . . Jimsonweed . . . Jameson . . . Jameston . . . Jamestown Weed. Yes! With a wild leap of joy, it finally came to me. The berries of this plant had caused mass poisonings in the colony at Jamestown, Virginia. This native American plant grew in the solarium. It caused eyes to become bright and the pupils to dilate if the handler touched his eyes.

Hadn't I seen Friedericke's eyes unnaturally bright? Weren't my own?

The lantern's light touched upon something else on the floor. I bent over. It was a book, a ledger of sorts amid the rubble.

The writing in it was a minuscule scrawl, like that in the frightening notes!

I sensed a presence behind me.

"Stay as you are," an angry voice grated.

Without turning, I knew who spoke.

† Chapter Fourteen

"I'll take that ledger." The voice was flat, toneless; its despairing, lifeless quality struck cold terror in my heart.

I did not move. Could not. Was afraid to.

"Hand it to me." The command was taut, strained.

I heard feet shifting uncertainly behind me. When I turned, I faced the hard, cold barrel of a gun.

"That's right, give it over." The words were steely now.

I hesitated. The black book was my only hope in this dastardly situation. If I gave it up, I would relinquish the tiny bit of leverage I had. With a boldness I did not know I possessed, I opened the small ledger to page upon page of debits and credits. "Whose records are these? Yours, Friedericke?"

The woman's mirthless laugh rose to fill the emptiness of the cave. "Nay, not mine alone."

"Iris'?" I ventured, for I was beginning to piece together a plan of monstrous deception.

The gun in her pudgy hand trembled at the mention of her beloved niece's name. "You are quick to catch on, Miss Hopkins. We surmised as much from the beginning and tried to induce you to leave."

"The threatening notes were hardly an inducement."

"An encouragement, then, just like this gun." I felt the weapon's icy prod at my temple, and I shivered. Satisfied,

191

Friedericke continued. "We could not have anyone here who was knowledgeable in medicine or problems of the mind. You are familiar with both. You started to snoop." She smiled malevolently. "And brought on your own demise."

"No. My death, like Herr Kirsch's and the others', will be on your head." I looked quickly at the broken apparatus on the floor, the makeshift machine used to extract the poison from its source. "You used the jimsonweed, didn't you?"

"Yes." A sly smile curled her lips. "Clever, wasn't it, to have a poison that mocked the very symptoms of the mental deterioration of certain patients?" She shook a finger warningly. "Don't think for a moment the victims weren't selected with care."

"Why? Why did you do it?" I got to my feet.

Friedericke looked momentarily puzzled. "For the money, of course."

Now it was my turn to be confused. "Money?"

The matron's tone turned venomous. "This house was the home of my youth. It was a magnificent mansion then, a resort for the wealthy. We had a grand time growing up here." Her voice shook with fury. "But *he* changed all that."

"Who?"

"My brother, Franz Joseph," she answered caustically. "He changed this lovely house into a retreat for the demented misfits of society. I had to get away. Iris wanted to move to the Ringstrasse. But we needed more money than Franz and Maximillian gave us." She went on, obviously pleased with herself. "You see, the families of the patients here have to pay a large, non-refundable fee before they can be accepted for admission. I convinced my brother to put an account in my name for the Ringstrasse house, and much of the money he got from these people he initially put into the Ringstrasse account. But nice things are very expensive . . . so Iris and I often paid the contractors before they sent bills for the extras here to the house. This way,

Maximillian and Franz never knew how much we spent." She glanced at my hand. "It's all there in the book. Now give it to me."

I was stunned, only dimly aware that Friedericke removed the evidence from my relaxed grip. "But why did you kill these poor people?"

"For a smart woman you sound incredibly stupid, Emily. If they died not too long after their arrival, we'd have the money without the expense of their care."

"Did Dr. Demel know this?"

"No. And I intend to keep it that way." The gun waved toward me again.

Nevertheless, I said my piece. "Not everyone here is wealthy. Don't you know that people pool their family resources to send a loved one to a private sanitarium to get well? These families needed relief. Caring for a sick one at home takes its toll on all family members. Those families were desperate." My voice rose. "How could you hurt them emotionally and financially?"

"We gave the patients something," Friedericke replied hotly, her jowls quivering. "We gave them *my* house to live in, luxuries they'd never known. Maids, fancy foods—"

"You killed them!" I screamed.

To my continued disbelief, the dowager shrugged, then added almost philosophically, "Isn't death the very goal of life, Emily?"

These last comments showed how skewed her thinking was, and again I felt fear's black grip. I had said enough. I should have remained silent and not upset her, but I could not school myself to do so. Besides, I was curious. "Why isn't Iris here to share your triumph?" I asked.

Friedericke's eyes glowed as bright as jewels, as dark as death. "*That's* the tragedy," she whispered. I could have sworn that her eyes filled up as she explained, "Iris told me you were Johann's lover. So I thought you were in his room that night, not Iris. I gave him the wine, knowing he never drank, and I thought he would serve the wine to *you*. Pity it didn't work."

"So Iris did herself in," I said, immediately wishing I could bite back the words.

"Shut up," snapped my captor, "and move toward the door."

I had traveled a long road up to this point. My stay in Vienna had been fraught with danger and obstacles since my arrival. But I felt I had looked fear and adversity in the face here, in this house, and become the victor over them. "What do you intend to do?"

Fine pearls of moisture dotted her upper lip. "We're going for our little walk now."

"Where?"

"To the pond," she snapped. "You'll have an accident there."

"You'll never get away with this."

"We'll see."

I stooped to pick up my reticule, for in it I had the third threatening note. This, and the others, had mentioned a horn. I pictured Friedericke's solarium. The poisonous jimsonweed. Devil's trumpet, it was called. I thought of Frau Steinmetz embroidering those trumpet-like flowers, of the other helpless innocents trapped in this terrifying house. Some of them suspected the foulness of what was going on around them. And they had tried to warn me.

We were near the old wooden door when I turned to Friedericke. "Did you destroy your chemical apparatus out of rage? Grief?"

She poked me in the ribs with her gun. "Up these steps," she barked, licking the sweat from her lips.

The afternoon sun was waning, giving way to that ghostly twilight. All the long walk to the duck pond I thought of Maximillian. I thought of our love . . . soon to be lost. It seemed incredible to me that I could finally muster the strength to fight for what I wanted, only to have it snatched miserably from me—as it was once before in my life. I wondered how often people had to suffer at the hand of some sly thief, or devil, or witch.

For greed! That always seemed to be at the root of evil schemes.

My reverie was broken by voices up ahead. I turned and saw Friedericke blanch, watched her hide the gun within the folds of her cloak.

"Don't do anything out of the ordinary," she hissed.

And then they were upon me. Demel, Max, Peter, and Herman, his duck. Maximillian threw up his arms in relief. "We've looked all over the woods for you. Thank God we found you."

Peter came over to take my hand. Fearful of having him so close to the gun, I stepped away. Friedericke followed. I glanced at Max, at his face, and saw the puzzlement in his eyes.

Not wanting to communicate anything, I looked away—at the duck who had wandered next to Friedericke. I watched her sharp little boot try to shoo the animal away, but he wouldn't go.

Friedericke laughed hollowly. Again came her swift kick, and it found its mark.

An angry squawk escaped the duck. He puckered his bill, stamped his feet, and snorted, as loud as any bovine.

"Damn thing is always in the wrong place," Friedericke snarled.

I heard Herman's quack, watched him fluff his feathers and fly near his tormentor's face.

Friedericke stepped back. The gun whipped up, then aimed at me.

At precisely that instant, someone else, someone who looked vaguely familiar to me, came out from behind a bush. "*Die Presse. Die Presse*," he shouted, marching stiffly over to Demel. "Professor Doctor," he cried, pointing to me. "Is *this* how you treat your patients?"

My heart was pounding. I wished desperately for my loved ones' safety, for this to be over. The gun went off. Peter screamed. My blood ran cold.

Maximillian's fingers gripped my shoulders, forcing me to

huddle with his son on the ground. I heard another shot and a splash. I saw the wild-eyed Dr. Demel stare disbelievingly into the pond.

He, Maximillian, and Herr Aschoff from the press immediately fished Friedericke's body from the water while I walked back to the house with Peter.

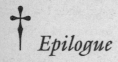
Epilogue

A month after the double funeral, Maximillian and I were privately married.

The parts of Friedericke's ledger that remained dry, the flasks and stove, the plants in the solarium, and the patients themselves gave the newspaper columns a degree of hysteria and sensationalism that rivaled fiction. For weeks, new developments in the case were blown up, stretched, and distorted in ugly headlines. At times not even I recognized the facts.

I had witnessed all this once before, of course. But the more I thought about it after the debacle at Demel house, the more I realized how fragile truth is, how easily it can be altered and exploited by any self-serving interest or wagging tongue. Iris' manipulation of the truth, her deliberate lie that I was Johann's mistress, led to her death. And Friedericke's deception brought about her demise. Each received her just desserts, I thought.

And Demel?

He'd once told me, "I deceive, Miss Hopkins, less than I am deceived." At the time I did not know what to make of that remark, nor could I have guessed what falseness may have nurtured it; but the statement proved to be prophetic. The man's own sister and niece had been cheating him and counteracting what he was trying to achieve at the sanitarium. Apparently he was just beginning to grasp the possibility of treachery sometime after I arrived there. My shock and anger at the extreme measures he took to ensure my silence have abated. In the end, he apologized and explained to me that he had never been a man of moderation, that he had been desperate, panicked, and driven to fury that dreadful night I was in his study.

The appearance that very evening of Herr Aschoff, the news reporter, was not due to Werner's prompting, but to the rumors circulating about the clinic. Werner had kept his word to me, and, to his gain, the sanitarium was sold, as was the Ringstrasse house. The tragic Dr. Demel was fined and sent to prison, where he died a broken man. I felt sorry for him, but I was pleased my father's biography passed from his hands to Maximillian's.

We live now in our own cozy Biedermeier house in the wooded hills of the Wienerwald. Peter, of course, is with us. Gone are his nightmares, his fear of food, and his unrelenting shock and sorrow at the events he was exposed to in that house of evil. He confided to us that he had seen a patient vomit, then had heard the next day that the man had died. He had seen someone mixing potions in the cellars, and he had received a threatening note that cautioned him about his own food if he were to speak up. That's why he only ate outside the house, or if the food was just from the oven. Did he know he was protecting his mother and his great aunt? We doubted it. The unknown demon can take on frightening proportions in someone's mind—though I think Iris' behavior would rank with the darkest imaginings of any tortured soul.

But Peter is mostly recovered, filled out, and as sensitive and kind as he always was. He brought Herman with him to the Biedermeier house and, after a few months, we changed the duck's name to Heroine, a name more appropriate to her theatrics at the pond, and to the constant attention she gave to the seven little ones who paddled blissfully behind her in her new quarters.

It is early morning, and the spring air is delicately seasoned with blossom and birdsong. Peter is at the stream catching what we hope will be our midday meal.

I am sitting on the edge of the bed, about to touch my feet to the floor when Maximillian's strong arm circles my waist and gathers me to his lean body.

"And how can I please you, Frau Doctor?"

I look into eyes that are bluer than blue. "Do you write the prescriptions or fill them, Herr Doctor?"

"I," he says, blatantly bragging, "can do both."

"What I would wish for, then, is a baby daughter, a wonderful little girl, all pink and white, with dark, dark hair."

The blue of his eyes flamed all the brighter. "What pleasure. What sweet, sweet pleasure."

A NOTE FROM THE AUTHOR

Dear Reader:

With Vienna's twilight splendor as the story's social and historical backdrop, and an asylum in the Viennese woods as its specific setting, I hope this gothic tale has given you as much enjoyment as I had researching and writing it.

While Dr. Demel's asylum never existed, it is based on Europe's long tradition of sanitaria. Similarly the Philadelphia Hospital is fictional. Dr. Kirkbride, by contrast, was the first superintendent of the Hospital for the Insane, now known as the Institute of the Pennsylvania Hospital, in Philadelphia, PA. His progressive approach to psychiatric care had far-reaching consequences.

It is also interesting to note that glass-domed mechanical pieces were quite popular in the late Victorian period. A mechanical orchestra performed in the Prater and thrill-seeking youths lined up for jolts of electricity, as described. Sarah Bernhardt was considered the darling of Vienna in the fall of 1888, and an English traveler writing at that time mentioned a dog so closely shaven it appeared "blue."

How could I have excluded that?

For color and clever hyperbole, Vienna's classified ads outdo any personals we read in our papers and magazines today. And, yes, Iris is the goddess of rainbows.

The rest, dear reader, is a dreamer's fancy.

CATHERINE RIEGER
Bryn Mawr, Pennsylvania